DISTANCE

Colin Thubron is the author of several classic masterpieces of travel writing, including *Among the Russians*, *The Lost Heart of Asia* and *In Siberia*. His fiction titles include *A Cruel Madness* (winner of the 1985 Silver Pen Award), *Falling*, *Emperor*, *Turning Back the Sun* and, most recently, *To the Last City*.

COLIN THUBRON

Distance

VINTAGE BOOKS
London

Published by Vintage 2006

2 4 6 8 10 9 7 5 3 1

The author thanks the following for permission to quote from
copyright material: Edward Arnold for W. MacNeile Dixon's *The
Human Situation* (1937); Penguin Books Ltd for *Selected Poems:
Yevtushenko*, translated by Robert Milner-Gulland and Peter Levi
(1962); and Verso for Paul Feyerabend's *Against Method* (1978)

First published in Great Britain in 1996 by
William Heinemann

Vintage
Random House, 20 Vauxhall Bridge Road,
London SW1V 2SA

Random House Australia (Pty) Limited
20 Alfred Street, Milsons Point, Sydney,
New South Wales 2061, Australia

Random House New Zealand Limited
18 Poland Road, Glenfield, Auckland 10, New Zealand

Random House (Pty) Limited
Isle of Houghton, Corner of Boundary Road & Carse O'Gowrie,
Houghton, 2198, South Africa

Random House Publishers India Private Limited
301 World Trade Tower, Hotel Intercontinental Grand Complex,
Barakhamba Lane, New Delhi 110 001, India

The Random House Group Limited Reg. No. 954009
www.randomhouse.co.uk/vintage

A CIP catalogue record for this book
is available from the British Library

ISBN 9780099459279 (from Jan 2007)
ISBN 0099459272

Papers used by Random House are natural,
recyclable products made from wood grown in
sustainable forests. The manufacturing processes
conform to the environmental regulations of the
country of origin

Printed and bound in Great Britain by
Bookmarque Ltd, Croydon, Surrey

For Margreta de Grazia

1

The first thing I notice is the hand resting on the tablecloth. It is lean, almost delicate. I move it a little, to be sure it is mine. Its fingers withdraw from a drained coffee-cup and a crumpled napkin. The only sounds in the restaurant are the clinking of knives and a child coughing. I look up. I cannot remember what I have eaten. I can hear my heart. An ornamental fig-tree makes a cascade by the window. Beyond it I can see shops in the street, clouded sunlight.

I feel light and empty. A ghost might feel like this. The knuckles of the hand are webbed by faint lines new to me. I wait for something to change. This can't last, I think, it's just for a minute. In a minute I'll be myself again. Behind me a family is eating: a robust young man and a younger woman, concentrating on their food. Only their child turns a white face and stares at me. She has beautiful pale eyes. I look away again. I think: if somebody speaks to me, I'll splinter.

Then the words gather in my head, and I try them out: *My memory's gone.*

I think my heart is dying down now. Perhaps this happened yesterday, or just an hour ago. Perhaps outside, on a department store rooftop, a surveillance camera caught the moment: a man walking purposefully, until suddenly, for no visible reason, he gave a start, and continued like a robot,

1

disappeared out of the lens . . . . But that's not how it feels. It feels as if I had been lost – or wandering somewhere – for a long time, and that only now have I returned to what I used to be. Yet all the pictures in my past are dim, as though the people who inhabit them must by now be old or dead. I glance at my hands again: but they are still a young man's. Yet I feel as if half of me is not here. Everybody else is more solid than I am. I'm trembling.

The waitress puts on the table a bill for ravioli and coffee, and I fumble automatically for my wallet. I squeeze its frayed and burnished leather in remembrance. It is more worn than I recall (the edges unstitching) but mine. Inside are several tenners and an identity card for the observatory where I work. So I do, I still do. My hands tremble through my pockets for anything else. There's a handkerchief, an unfamiliar pen, a car-key labelled 'Honda', a letter. Beneath my name on the envelope is an address I do not recognise, a cottage in a Dorset village. I cannot imagine it. I never craved that kind of peace. The letter shakes in my hand. When I unfold it I find it dated 'April 20th', without a year. It comes from an old friend. He's sorry we have fallen so much out of touch, he writes. He has become a postulant in an Anglican religious order, and perhaps – between his seminars and retreats – I'll visit him? I remember him all right, years ago; he was worldly and un-clouded, recalling nothing which might have prompted this.

Is everybody, then, losing their mind? Gingerly I stand up, half expecting to fall. My footsteps hesitate over the tiled floor. I push open the door into the lavatory, imagining that everyone is watching me. Then I'm alone. Above the wash-basin hangs a half-length mirror, but for the moment I'm afraid to approach it. I stand just outside its vision, feeling sick, and the fantastic notion occurs to me that if I face it I may see nobody at all. So I try to locate my last memory, but cannot tell how long ago it was. Two years, three? And I do not know when now is.

I steady my mind. In my inside pocket the postmark on the envelope gives me the year. I read but cannot quite grasp it. That year, for me, hovers emptily in the future. It is not unimaginably far, just beyond the range of my inhabiting. Yet I am living in it.

I hunt in my past for what is closest. I remember the collapse of the Soviet Union, my posting to Brabourne Observatory, the launch of the Hubble Space Telescope, the Gulf War, a scattering of personal, dateless things . . . .

Then I edge into the mirror. I see a face of frozen lines pouring from its mouth and cheeks. Its lower lip is bitten in. Its eyes are wide and inflamed. I have to calm it into ordinariness, smooth it in my hands. Then I cover it over, my eyes, my forehead, and look again. The face seems not exactly older. Its hair is still chestnut-coloured and its features – the wide forehead tapering to a stubborn mouth and chin – become familiar as I watch. It strikes me as intense, somehow selfish, with a touch, perhaps, of suppressed tenderness. But something has changed and I do not know what it is. I think it is my eyes. Some look – expectancy, future – is no longer there. They look sightless, like blue stones. It is strange. I wonder if I imagine it. I try smiling at myself in greeting, and the lips curl sardonically. I draw my hand down my face again to wipe it clean.

3

Are these, then, the eyes you gazed into, the lips you kissed?

But perhaps I'm mistaken. I am not, after all, myself. I turn my back on the mirror and make for the exit. The waitress smiles perfunctorily: no sign that the person who came in was any different from the one going out. The street is full of people under a worn sky. Nothing distinguishes it. The shops, the pubs, the offices: all seem placeless. Brick, glass, pale stone. For a moment I stay rooted to the sidewalk, listening to snatches of conversation, music. Then my feet start to walk of their own accord. I pass a bank, a supermarket, a washetaria. The window of the Oxfam shop says 'Spring is Here'. The crowds move around me on mysterious errands: workmen carrying things, women wheeling babies. Something elusive in their style has changed, their clothes and shoes more lumpy and garish. The eyes of one or two drift over me, and I feel this frailty fluttering high and light in my chest. I glimpse alleys, but I mustn't go down them or I will be lost. I stop on the pavement. Lost from where? I don't even know where this town is. In England, somewhere.

I sit on a bench so that nobody will notice me. That way the fear subsides a little. Only in my mind, I think, am I conspicuous. My face feels blank. My clothes are everyday: a denim jacket, a turtle-neck sweater, jeans. I don't recognise them, but their lack of style is mine.

A vagrant sits down beside me. His eyeballs are netted in blood. Perhaps he wants something. He lowers a beer can between his feet with a bandaged hand, and looks up at the sky. I feel closer to him than to any of these others: we are brothers in homelessness. I even want to take his damaged hand in mine. It seems a long time since I heard my own voice, but all at once it rasps out: 'What's this town called?'

He squints at me suspiciously, then laughs: 'This is fucking Moscow, mate.'

I begin to walk again, shakily, going back the way I came. I'm seeking out the restaurant again, as if it is the re-entry point to somewhere I've forgotten. On the way, in the window of an estate agent, I try to discover where I am. I study the announcements of desirable residences while a cat weaves back and forth over my shoes. Soon I understand that I'm in a town in Wiltshire, north of Salisbury Plain, where I've never been before. Yet the mewling of the cat around my ankles gives me the idea that it knows me, and I even follow it while it calls and turns its head. A foolish hope rises in me. Then the cat twists down an alley and is gone, leaving me absurdly bereft. I think: Christ, this town must have a clinic I can go to, a hospital, anywhere.

I walk, looking for signs. Back past the Methodist chapel, a video shop, the restaurant. Then I come upon my car. I would know it any-where – it has a comically twisted aerial – and I feel a rush of affection for it. My key fumbles in the door, and it opens. Sitting inside, gazing across its dashboard, I find the glove compartment crammed with the same old maps and classical cassettes, and the faint carmine smear of a woman's make-up stains the passenger seat. There is a pair of spectacles too, and for a second I wonder whose they are. Then, tentatively, I lift them to my own face. Yes, I need them now.

From the milometer I see that I've driven over forty thousand miles since I think I remember.

Forty thousand! I try to imagine these journeys, the people and the places between them. And suddenly I'm weeping. The tears come in staccato chokes out of my stomach. I swallow them back like phlegm, but they come again. Yet I don't know if this is just frustration or if the tears are reacting to something I've forgotten, and they start to take on a ghastly life of their own – meaningless, hysterical – as though signalling some innate condition.

2

The words come thin, as though they might be lies: 'My name's Edward Sanders . . . I'm a postgraduate research student in astronomy. I live . . . .' I pause while the doctor writes it down. He looks uneasy: he's younger than I am – just a houseman in the casualty wing.

He asks: 'When did you remember what had happened? When did you "come to"?'

I feel momentarily embarrassed, as if this were a charade of someone else's making, or that we're acting in a fifth-rate movie. I glance at my wrist and see a watch I do not recognise. 'Two and a half hours ago. It was like . . . .'

'Yes?'

'Like waking up. As if I'd been sleep-walking.'

He writes things on his pad. His face is long and angular under a shock of ginger hair. He watches me with his head half averted, perhaps suspicious. 'Do you feel any pain?'

'No . . . .' Only this cold lightness about myself, as if memories were weights now gone.

'No bruising? Abrasions?' He stands up and moves behind my chair. 'Sometimes people sustain head injuries which numb . . . .' His fingertips start to probe along my scalp. 'Have you ever suffered concussion?'

'Once. But years ago, ten years. In a car crash.'

'Did you experience any memory loss?'

7

'No, nothing.' That is the irony. At university my memory was considered rather extraordinary. I knew Schrödinger's wave equation by heart. The doctor is probing along my hairline now, like a dentist hunting for cavities.

'Tell me if it hurts.'

But I feel only a faint hope, as if his fingers might transmit remembrance. I try to help him, to think back a day ago, then a week. But it's like staring at mist. I recall the sensation of burning at my confirmation, as the bishop touched my head and channelled holiness into it. And now the doctor is asking about my next of kin – as if I were a corpse – about my parents, my employers. He is seated in front of me again, and all the time watching me with his foxy eyes, uncertain. 'How long ago is your last memory?'

I think I'm sweating. I feel absurdly like a criminal. I've already strained to locate this memory. But everything seems to stop short more than two years ago. Before then the years seem familiar and inhabited, and I can find events. Afterwards they are meaningless, like the date postmarked on the envelope. It's as if they're waiting to happen to me. It sounds childish, but I say: 'My mother's birthdays were a kind of family reunion, in late April. The last one I remember was two years ago.'

He is making notes again. 'And what do you recollect about the months before? Was there stress? Unhappiness?'

'Isn't there always?'

'Not for everyone.'

But when I recall that time it doesn't exhale anything. The tension I feel reverberates from somewhere else. I can't describe it. It's as if some-

8

thing were pressing up beneath my skull. It even
has a physical presence: here, between my eyes,
throbbing. (Can he see it?) It doesn't belong in any
year that I remember, no. It belongs later.

'Relax, Mr Sanders.'

'I'll relax when I find myself again.' I don't like
this man. I suspect he doesn't believe me. 'What's
going to happen?'

'It's impossible to be certain.' He's looking at me
hard, perhaps to see how much I can take. 'But
you seem to be suffering from a retrograde
amnesia. Memory usually comes back within a
few days, or weeks at most. More than that I can't
tell you. I'm referring you to a specialist.'

'How does it come back then? Do I just wait?'

'It will probably return in fragments, quite
naturally. The earlier memories generally return
first. The amnesia shrinks, as it were. Part of your
bewilderment now is because you've been in what
we call a fugue state – wandering. Quite sane, but
wandering maybe for several days.'

'Why? Why does this happen?' I sound angry.

'Maybe through an accident, a blow to the head.
But your condition seems to be psychological. I
don't know this, I'm not a specialist, but these
kinds of amnesia usually arise from stress. From
something intolerable.'

The throbbing between my eyes starts up
again. My mind gropes after whatever might
have happened to me, meets a blank. He's looking at me more askance than ever. I just say: 'I'm
not sure.'

'Were you ever under psychoanalysis?'

'I never had any time for that.'

'Perhaps in your work . . . there were difficul-
ties?'

My work: how strange. It's only now I realise that over two years' research has disappeared overnight – not from astrophysics (it is all notated) but from my own consciousness. I cannot grasp this yet. But I have the feeling that I was on the brink of some greater understanding: something not momentous, but important in its way, something I will never now grasp. For the moment, at least, it seems a small tragedy.

The doctor goes on: 'What does your work consist of?'

'It's the study of black holes.'

'Black holes . . . .' He's looking foxy again, as if it might be a joke.

I try to explain, while a tiny knot pinches his forehead. And as I do so a little of the wonder of it comes back to me, as if I were a student again. Maybe it's the hunched incomprehension of this man, his ingrained distrust, but I want to make him feel it too, although I've never felt evangelical about astronomy. It's a science, after all. Yet now the obscure beauty of what I do returns to me, as I try to explain – in faltering images – about black holes, and a casualty screams far down the hospital corridor.

They are the ghosts that haunt our universe (I start to tell him) – the core of massive stars that have died, collapsed in on themselves aeons ago and shrunk to nuggets of near-infinite density. The whole mass of Earth, under the conditions of this death, would be compressed to a body with the value of less than a centimetre. Yet black holes may exist as massive as a thousand billion Suns. So great is their gravitational pull that they bend space and light-rays around them until they become a hecatomb of gas, stars, dust, light, which are sucked inside them and sealed off from the outer world for ever.

Even the absoluteness of Time vanishes here. To an outside observer, a human body falling into a black hole would plunge down a curvature of space-time where the minutes slowed to nothing until he hung timeless and for ever in the disc of the vortex. Inside, the density of matter becomes infinite. Time has stopped, and all known laws break down.

These black holes infest the universe. They may outnumber even the living stars. In fact they may constitute the heart of every star-system. A black hole with a mass a hundred thousand times that of the Sun probably lurks in the centre of our own galaxy. Yet sometimes to me these dark stars seem to be less material phenomena than regions of pure mathematics. An astronomer once called them the most perfect macrocosmic bodies in the universe, because they are invisible – formed only from our concepts of space and time.

The doctor sits there without expression. I don't think he's listened to a damn thing. And now he spits out these little questions, like owl-pellets: 'What kind of tensions does this work impose?' and adds: 'Do you get eye-strain?'

In the antiseptic hush of the hospital my laughter erupts in a terrible bark. It's the popular concept of us, I know: that we spend the night gazing through telescopes at the heavens. But I feel tired now, and want to end this farce. I say, to bore him: 'It's mostly radio-astronomy these days, collecting signals. Black holes give out X-ray emissions which you can't even detect from the ground. There's too much pollution. So my data comes from satellite telescopes programmed in

Germany. It arrives as a string of digits on a video-cassette.'

'There must have been something else in your life.' He seems to pity me.

Yes, I think, there must have been. He means women, of course. But five years ago I remember things simplifying and realigning. As my affair with Cassie began to wane, she fell into the arms of her boss and married him, leaving our mutual debt of sadness and recrimination oddly unpaid. At her wedding, before she drove away, she tossed me her bouquet of orange blossom, and neither of us regretted anything.

Then the mass and velocity of a black hole in the constellation Monaceros hijacked two years of my life. And after that, oh yes, I had everything planned. I would secure a new position at Jodrell Bank or Cambridge. I would probably marry in my mid-thirties. Then . . . I can't remember.

While I recount all this the doctor, of course, just sits there haloed in his white coat and super-cilious air of knowledge. If he thinks that a black hole is an apt symbol for my life, he doesn't say so. But he clings like a bulldog to his Freudian agenda. Am I an only child? Do I come from a broken home? When at last he echoes: 'So you enjoyed a decent, stable family life,' it sounds cynical.

Or perhaps I imagined that.

Now he says: 'But something else was wrong, wasn't it?'

'I don't know.' I stare down at myself. Am I still sweating? 'Maybe nothing's wrong.' I clamp my hands together. 'Maybe I've just got a virus. I've heard of viruses that attack the brain.'

That, perhaps, is why I can't reassemble her. She

12

slides in and out of focus. More like a force. Wide, fine eyes.

I say: 'You'd think your strength of feeling would bring somebody back, wouldn't you? Instead it's as if they're dead.'

'It doesn't work like that. Even the order memories return in doesn't seem to depend on their importance . . . .'

Well, hell, do I just wait? Everyone else I love is here: my reticent father, my monolith of a mother, Cassie. Only this other woman falls inside the wrong years, and escapes. And I was never good at waiting. I think I'm frightened you're dead. I could bring you back if I remembered you. But it's probably useless to force memories. My forehead's pulsing again. 'Yes, there was someone.' You must be hunting for me by now. You'll be worried.

'Who?'

'I don't remember. I just know there was.' Am I on a register of missing persons?

He's looking at me sideways again. I see only one green eye, as if he's holding the other in reserve. Perhaps he thinks this is my way of walking out on a bad marriage.

'Were you happy?'

'That's not the point.'

Was I? I stand up, surprising us both. There's nothing he can do for me.

'I'm referring you to our neurologist. Will you wait back at reception? It won't be ten minutes.'

'Yes, yes.' But I won't. These people can't do a bloody thing. They're less doctors than inquisitors, and already he's wheeled out too many addresses from me: my parents, my GP. If there's anything to find out, I'll find it out myself, alone. Anyway, after I reach reception, I slip out unnoticed. I'm going back.

When I set eyes on you, I'll remember.

3

As the road turns south, the hills of the Purbeck peninsula light up with gorse and heather, and start rolling towards the sea. It will soon be evening. My car runs smooth, but when I press the accelerator it hardly responds, as if it's forgotten me. I don't remember this land. I wait for something to ignite my recognition – the Saxon earthworks round Wareham, the shattered pinnacles of Corfe Castle – but nothing does. Beyond a limestone village strange to me, the track to my home begins its descent. Nothing's like I imagined. The cottage named on the envelope is so secluded that I crunch down the track for half a mile and it's still invisible. Then its name appears, carved vertically down a gatepost, as if in Chinese characters.

I can't believe I live here, no; this must be hers. I park the car outside. The evening light falls honeyed and unreal. I push the iron gate. It whimpers on its hinges. Air fans up cold in my chest. Should I turn back? If I wait a day, go to a hotel, my memory may return. But my feet start walking almost on tiptoe along the drive. The only sound is the whine of bluebottles in the bare blackberry bushes. I follow the pale-earthed drive between ash trees. It's corrugated by tyre-tracks. Young nettles are breaking through its stones.

Then I turn the corner, and the cottage meets

me four-square in blazing white stucco. Its roof-tiles make a steep cascade half way to the ground. Beyond it the hedgerows are white with hawthorn. Above it a faint moon already imprints the sky, and a jet fighter has left a soundless thread of smoke.

As I walk on, it stays unknown to me. I'm sure it wasn't I who stacked up the firewood near the dustbins, or piled the seashells and broken fossils along a window-ledge. My feet rasp on the threshold. I stop, trying to visualise her, can't. Blonde-streaked hair . . . . But my imagination works fatally. I remember images I've conjured before, and they take on truth. I remember imaginary memories. Somewhere water is trickling under the brambles.

When I ring the bell it sounds far inside, waking no recollection. Nothing. For an instant I imagine my forgotten self emerging to greet me. But no one comes, and I have no key. I go round to the back and tug at the doors of a little built-out orangery until they open.

How strange. I wait on the step for a hint of foreknowledge, the feeling that whatever I will find I will have seen before, but it does not come. My overcoat is hanging on a hook inside. The air presses stale and warm as I step through a thicket of geraniums. It is a cavernous kitchen, filled with the last sunlight and sharp, herbal scents. Against the whitewashed walls the stripped pine shelves and dressers glow with unfamiliar pottery – yellow and blue – interspersed by Japanese lacquerware and a confusion of curios which look picked up for a song or plucked off the beach: *azulejo* tiles, drift-wood and dried starfish, a rosewood tea-caddy, a wickerwork badger, conch shells, onyx, a brass

16

clock-face with a half-obliterated smile. But the briefcase in the corner is mine, and one of my pullovers is lying over a chair. Two up-ended wine-racks and a crimson-painted chest bristle with dried flowers, and other shelves swarm with labelled pots: stem ginger chutney . . . blackberry vinegar . . . juniper berries.

Against this musty intimacy the floor is flagged austerely in local stone, the ceiling hung with a rank of spotlights, and high on the walls, between posters of modern art exhibitions, a series of abstract canvases makes a stark, cerebral intrusion. In the bookshelves my choice and some-one else's are helplessly interknit: Fred Hoyle's *The Frontiers of Astronomy* alongside Gombrich's *Art and Illusion*.

Then, on the supper table, I see a note written in a rhythmic, unknown hand. *Darling, Naylor's portrait is going to take longer than I thought, so I won't be back from Lewes until Friday afternoon. Hell. If you need me, I'll be staying there. I only hope your trip went well. My love, Naomi. PS The owl is back.*

It burns in the dying sunlight. So that is her name: Naomi. I listen to it in my head. Three vowels which recreate nothing. There are two days before she returns. I try out the word softly: 'Naomi'. It arrives as a desolate whisper. Even her name, gone.

My feet tap across the flagstones, up and down. If I stare long and hard enough, this room may re-focus into a room I remember. I open cupboard doors hoping the things inside will be shimmering with past life. What did I do here? What did we say? It's like a vacant stage, but I'm afraid to people it in case invented memories block off real ones. Instead I must try to create gaps, emptiness.

17

But the pinewood chairs invite the images of the people who sat in them. So does the sofa, whose cushions are indented with the ghost of someone's back. What friends do we have? I go and sit in the orangery alcove in the chair which I imagine was mine (bare, high-backed) and gaze at the one opposite. We must have talked here often. Her chair has patinated wood, beautiful, and worn arm-rests (I touch them). But after a while the blaze of Matisse colours and the dry, Mediterranean glare of the geraniums exist so strongly in the present that they pre-empt any memory of themselves. There is no gap for the past to seep into. I think: better to inhabit a neutral space, cover the eyes, wait.

I open the door into a short passageway. It has whitewashed walls and a cord carpet. At once I start to imagine people there: her, me. We stroll from room to room, chatting, switching lights on and off, without looking to see if one another's there, because we know we are. Through a door on the right I glimpse a small studio. I creep in like a trespasser. A frosted skylight disseminates the dusk in an even pallor over the room. The walls are bare brick – pale like the earth of all this region, it seems – and the windows shut with blinds. Fallen specks of oil-paint freckle the easel, the stool, even the tiled floor, in a prismatic rain. A dresser is crowded with paint-tubes and stone jars sprout sable and bristle brushes. Between them some scattered ink drawings, apparently done at random, show hands – several of them skeletal – in different postures of repose. I sift them in ignorance, while she grows strange to me. Her palette rests on a shelf nearby. Around its rim the blobs of oil-paint shine still wet, circling from white through umber and siennas to lamp black and Prussian blue. It's as if she has just gone.

A canvas is wet too, still unfinished on her easel. It is the full-length portrait of a woman in middle-age. She stands in a high-collared dress with her hands clasped in front of her. The background is daubed in harsh grey strokes. There is no decoration of dress or gesture. Her face stares out in a Morse Code of dashed and dotted features: full but tight lips, severely parted hair, the hint of a double chin. The skin texture is yellow and pure. Faint highlights tauten the cheeks. At first I think the portrait only half complete. But after a while, looking, I wonder what is left to be done.

From a nearby rack I gingerly extract four or five other portraits. They all share the same uncompromising frontal pose, as if the sitter were staring alone into a mirror. The starkness of features repeats itself too, but with different effects. If there is any appendage – the spectacles on an old woman's lap, a dog-lead dangling from a girl's hand – it looks haunted by some undefined significance. The sitters seem to have passed into the linear economy of icons.

Then, with dawning alarm, I come upon two portraits of me. One looks ten years younger than the other, but of course it cannot be. I prop it on the easel. I am standing full-length. A red sweater and shock of chestnut hair enhance the feel of suppressed energy. My fists are clenched at my sides. It is a face of incongruous intensity. The brushstrokes round the strong chin and mouth quiver with impatience. She has found softness only in the watery highlights at the corners of the eyes, brimming with something like hurt, which the rest of the face repudiates.

The second portrait is shocking. How ill have I been, then? The change is secreted in the subtlety of her brushstrokes. I can scarcely define it. But I become aware of my face's bones. I am seated on the edge of a sofa, against a whitewashed wall. One hand lifts to my chest with splayed fingers. Some translucent pigment about the cheeks and forehead, or perhaps the wide, almost diamond stare of the eyes, steep this face in ambiguity.

How long must she have stood looking at me while painting, and I looking at her? It records a man reduced beyond love. Did I really look like that? (Do I still?) She has frozen my illness like a mortician. Perhaps it is only my own self-pity which makes me think its pigment includes: 'I love him. He is sick.'

It is the honesty which I remember in her, that unflinching gaze. The portraits are full of her stillness. Wide, grey eyes. It's not comfortable, that stare. I walk back to the kitchen, to calm myself. I try to deduce her from pottery, pictures, books. Did we buy this house together, or is it hers? Suddenly she's easier to feel now, her real warmth, her intelligence. I have the notion that she's just outside my vision, and that if I jerk my head round, or squint through half-closed eyes to the place where objects unfocus – I'll glimpse her.

Then the telephone shrills beside me. It trembles all through my body. For a moment I cannot conceive who it might be. It screams out of the present, where I don't belong. (But I will, I soon will.) My hand reaches out automatically, then withdraws. I force myself to sit down. It rings on and on. I wonder if it is Naomi, and suddenly I long to hear her speak. But my hands stay clamped under my armpits. I can't bear to hear the voice I won't recognise. I clasp the sides of my chair until the ringing stops.

Now I wonder if it was the observatory calling. How many days have I been absent? But Christ, I may no longer be working there. Somewhere, I imagine, in a hotel I've forgotten, a briefcase contains my diary and house-keys. (Perhaps they'll be returned to me one day.) But I remember my old work number. So I watch the phone, wondering if it will ring again, and if I will dare pick it up. Then, fumblingly, I dial. For a long time it rings while I imagine the approach of the night receptionist two years ago. When a voice answers, I do not recognise it. Frailly I ask to speak to myself. Her reply comes back light, girlish: 'Mr Sanders is on sick-leave. He won't be back for two weeks.'

A surge of relief floods through me: relief at the continuity of my own existence, in the same role, in the same place. 'Nothing serious, I hope?' I add, smiling to myself: 'He's an old friend.'

The voice tightens. 'I'm afraid that's all I know.'

I replace the receiver. The nightmare of my unemployment has dissolved so fast that I scarcely had time to fear it. Outside, the light has drained from the sky. Beyond our orchard, under the waxy moonlight, the hedgerows undulate in mists of hawthorn. I go to the end of the passage and into the bedroom. The double bed lies under a white duvet, and its little tables shine with the first disturbing intimacy: twin lamps, photographs of our parents. On hers: a pewter hedgehog, some face-cream, a novel. On mine: two history books, a burnt-down candle, an alarm clock. These objects – and her slippers discarded under the bed – evoke a pang of emptiness. I pick up the photo by her bedside and see a woman of about fifty –

her mother, I suppose – with dark eyes. I think: if these don't force remembrance, what will?

In our wardrobe my own casual clothes are unchanged, hanging beside her pullovers and jeans and a few smart, restrained suits and dresses – grey and white, black and white. And nothing means a thing. I feel no guilt at my intrusion, just this ache of loss, which is out of control now. Shamelessly I pull out her underpants, her bras, pleased by their white slenderness, and bury my face in them, and still they might be anyone's.

On her dressing-table a little throng of lipsticks and lotions (I wonder how much she took away with her?) stands among alabaster pots filled with hair-grips and pins. I think of her blonde streaks and am unsure even of this now. Searching for a strand of hair in her comb, I find none. I start to feel faintly sick. I lift up her hand-mirror, as if her face might be stamped there, and see only my harrowed features, her portrait . . . .

I must calm myself. I have two days, after all. Perhaps the night – unconsciousness – is kinder to the past. By morning . . . . Gently I unscrew the perfume bottle on her dressing-table – scent, the oldest mnemonic. And as I pass it beneath my nostrils, I believe I remember it – elusive, faintly woody – but from where I have no idea.

I replace the bottle gently, like a talisman. I feel a tinge of despair. I try to build her up by an accumulation of details – the simplicity of her ear-rings, the size of her shoes – as if this is all I will ever have. But she floats free of them. I open the bedside drawers and with detached curiosity finger the little card indented for her contraceptive pills, mostly gone. Beneath it is a birthday card on which two hedgehogs sleep in one another's arms.

It is inscribed to her by me.

Then, deliberately, in the hope that the most powerful intimacies must break through, I climb into my side of the bed, pulling the duvet to my shoulders, and gaze at the unfilled outline of her face on the pillow. My lips converge where hers should be. I shut my eyes against their absence. I try repeating angrily 'Naomi!' as if to bully her back. My palms, framing her face, cradle blank air. And suddenly it's frightening, the whiteness of the bed, and the telephone is ringing, jarring, from the room next door.

I move towards it into a small study, hoping the ringing will stop. Then I grasp the receiver before I have time to think. It is my father. His voice – guarded, a little querulous – seems to loop over the years to reach me. But as I listen, imbibing its familiar intonations, its habitual coughs and pauses, it reels me slowly, painlessly, into the present. He says that some hospital has been in touch with him, asking questions about me. Is it true about this amnesia? How much time have I lost then? He makes it sound permanent.

I say: 'Two years.'

The silence elongates, filled with something of his own. At last he says: 'You don't remember anything at all?'

'No.' I hear myself trying to add: 'Just . . . just . . . . I don't think so.'

'What about Naomi?'

'She's not here. She's away until Friday.'

'Away.' His tone is touched by consolation. It's not like him. 'You can't stay there alone, Eddy. Why not come up here for the day?' Then he stops, and I can hear the doubts opening in him. 'You do . . . remember how to get here?'

'Yes, of course!' I laugh, too loud. But I think: yes, better to be away from here. After I've left this place, it will come back to me. Memory sticks to wherever we are not. I say: 'Yes, I'll come, of course I'll come home. Tomorrow.' Yet I'm mortified. A grown man, I want my parents' comfort. I want the continuity of their love, which will have continued unchanged over the whited-out years. Tomorrow I'll recover it, like a thread, and I'll start to make the past again. Yes. I replace the receiver.

So I am sitting in my own study, at my own desk. I recognise the things around me: reference books, my word processor, crystal paperweights. But they seem cooled. They might have belonged to me long ago, and loosened their ties since. But they are still mine. The same dislocation haunts the letter on the desk-top. It is in my own hand-writing, half finished, thanking an acquaintance for a book (but I recall neither). The jagged vigour of my handwriting has run amok. It peters out in the page's whiteness.

I rummage through my drawers, where the few bundles of letters all belong to my farther past. But I come upon broken elastic bands, as if others had been thrown away. Then I find my photograph albums, but their holiday snapshots are sporadic – whole years go unrecorded – and when I reach the recent past I find that they have been torn out, eight pages of them, leaving rectangles of dried glue. All that is left are meaningless captions: 'Manadao . . . Sulawesi, Indonesia . . . .' Did I tear them out to send to someone? I can't imagine having been to Indonesia.

Then I come upon a drawer chaotic with my current preoccupations: articles cut out of journals, speculations on quasars and black holes –

jumbled in with frenetic calculations in my own handwriting. I look at them with dismay. None of them means anything to me now. Amongst them are sheets filled by strips of data from my exabyte tapes (I shouldn't have removed them from the observatory). But they seem to have been selected piecemeal, and my own notes veer into scrawled asides on unrelated topics: patterns of X-ray signals for neutron stars, even an abusive letter to NASA. It's as if I'd gone insane. I try to detect when these were written, and cannot tell. But they appear recent. Then I unearth a list of things my supervisor has said, with rude cartoons of one of my colleagues and some hypotheses about ionised gas clouds. I feel distantly appalled, as if they were the writings of someone else. What was I doing? Other notes are jotted down on scraps of paper and stapled to the rest.

At the bottom of the drawer is a quarter-filled notebook scribbled with miscellanea in the feverish hand which is like a caricature of my own. The writing deteriorates as it goes on – the last sentences are barely legible – and a few disconnected mathematical formulae intrude. I read it by the light of my old desk-lamp (this at least I remember) while I drop back into a mind I no longer recognise.

I'm sorry, Naomi, I didn't mean quite what I said. Perhaps we just see different colours. But how the fuck can you expect to understand me when you refuse to adopt my eyes? I'll try again. Look, I don't expect you to be a scientist, Christ, what a fate, it's just a matter of indulging your imagination in something bigger than oil-paints. You say I'm blinded by death, for the obvious reasons, but perhaps you're blinded by life.

Naomi: more than ninety per cent of the universe may be dead. The stars shrink into white dwarfs, black holes, red dwarfs, neutron stars, too faint, too cold. The energy radiates away as I talk to you. Not even helium burns for ever. From our own burnt-out star, we observe this. A hundred thousand million stars in our galaxy alone – and the black holes of the dead may outnumber them.

[Then comes detailed information on the accretion discs of various proposed black holes, where the language turns mathematical.]

We may observe the universe, but can never really touch it. The nearest likely source of life, in Alpha Centauri, is four light-years away, more than quarter of a million times farther than the Sun. Even if we had a transmitter capable of responding to signals from outer space, we'd almost certainly die waiting for a reply. Within the lifetime of any human being the simple question 'Who's there?' will never be answered.

And every moment the stars are leaving us. Our own superclusters of galaxies, with a diameter already of four million light-years, diffuse into space like dust.

So we grow lonelier.

There are galaxies detected so distant that they are a hundred million times fainter than the naked eye can see – and still they are flying away from us.

Yesterday you asked me about the future of the world, and I told you. You smiled and offered me coffee.

We witness only the past. Even the sunlight on your face, darling, is eight minutes old. The light that we receive from distant stars set out before our Earth existed.

If you're dead, why don't you forget me? I didn't mean that. But it can't matter. Senility wouldn't have suited you anyway. All that wasting and forgetting.

And in the end the stars will grow old and die. The nebulae will disperse, and energy fade away.

Over billions of years, matter itself will start to break

down, until the universe is a sea of radiation, and nothing will ever happen again. So we'll thin into uniformity (and I can't take your hand).

And if in the other scenario (there always is one) the gravitational pull of the infinitesimally thinned matter – you, me – is just enough, the universe will start violently to recollapse. Then the galaxies will reform for the Big Crunch, and the overheating sky will blaze with continuous daylight. Time will reverse, and I'll grow young with you. (I'm joking – but it would serve you right.) The Crunch has grandeur, after all. You'd adore that. Better to die young! Embrace suicide, drown in your own fire! Isn't it? Soon, in any case, the temperature of background radiation will tear the stars apart, and in the mass of collapsing debris the black holes will multiply and coalesce, engulfing everything, until the universe is sucked into a single chasm in which Time ends, perhaps, or creation starts again (and I still can't take your hand) and if you ever believed in anything, you . . . if you were only colour-blind, if that's all it was, then . . . . I can't ask your forgiveness . . . .

The last sentence is in tatters, and this babble is followed by excerpts from works on primitive stellar myths and such like, which string out into incoherence.

For the first time I feel afraid of my memory returning.

4

Now it is tomorrow, and nothing has changed. Sleep has just kept the house in the starkness of novelty. It's nineteen hours since my blackout lifted. I can face only my parents. Depressing, this intermittent calm I feel, as if I were starting to accept.

I leave the house behind with relief. Only the car surrounds me with myself. And now, seventy miles to the north, the country softens into memory, and the village of my childhood is folded into the Vale of Pewsey. The downs are speckled with Friesian cattle which loom in foreshortened perspective just behind the houses. I drive down the only street, a little afraid that this too-pretty tableau – the medley of house-fronts behind budding gardens, the Norman church, the half-timbered pub – will suddenly go cold and back out of my memory. But it consoles me as if I were a child. It's peopled by parishioners half a generation back, and I remember them: farmers and schoolteachers, shopkeepers and widows, a priest, a retired colonel, a solicitor. It rests in the time-warp of my adolescence. I have left it behind; but I feel a deep, residual possessiveness, which does not allow it to change. For a second I consider going into the pub, then imagine some family acquaintance approaching me. 'It's Eddy, isn't it? Down to see your parents then? What have you been doing recently?'

I don't know, *I don't know*. 'Oh, the same old thing.'

'Found anything yet? Seen anything new?'

'No, not really.' For all I know I've discovered life on Alpha Centauri.

I pass the green with the First World War memorial, the village shop where everything's stale (my mother says), the sleepy garage. Then I'm through the village proper and glimpse the farm whose horses I used to ride over the downs. Next comes the haunted rectory where in my childhood the owner held a ghost-viewing party and appeared shrouded in a sheet – Woooh! Woooh! – as the church clock struck and we squealed in terror. And beyond is my home – the only one I know for now – a converted farmhouse standing among oak trees.

I open the gate with mixed estrangement and relief. It seems years ago that I was here. The hazel and yew hedges, the strip borders, are all in place. But in the twenty yards between garden gate and front door, walking down the brick path, I realise that something is different. It's indefinable – like the instinct which first tells an art expert that a picture is a fake – but it's palpable wherever I turn. The design of the plants already vivid in April – the gold-green philipendula against the dark myrtle, the spread of the tree-peony above the delphiniums, all the subtle, contrasting textures which my mother has nurtured – have shifted out of true. Bindweed is growing under the hedges.

Even before I've reached the door, the presentiment has opened a pit in my stomach. I cannot press the bell. For an instant I want to stay in the garden, as if by refusing to cross the threshold I might halt time, and this foreboding will melt away. I peer through a window into the hall. It's dark. Dimly I can make out on one wall the long-exposure photographs of stars which my father framed there, and which so excited me as a boy: the Carina nebula like a celestial oil-field ablaze, the mystifying blue headlamps of the Pleiades. They are distantly comforting. And now I step under the porch, and my hand is at the bell, which tinkles far inside, and I cannot help imagining my mother turning from the stove or sink, her face lifted and flushed in anticipation, and the collies trooping after her towards me.

But the door opens abruptly as if my father had been hovering close against it, and at once I see in his face everything I have to know, and when I take him in my arms his depletion is tangible there – the jut of his shoulder-blades, the faint wobble in his legs – so that although he is only sixty-seven I think: how long will he last?

He steps back to let me in. Behind their spectacles his eyes wander palely over mine, not knowing where to stop. In any case, I cannot meet them. I just want him to say: 'She's out walking the dogs' or 'She'll be in the orchard'.

Instead we perch opposite one another in the sitting-room, and talk by a code of commonplaces, steeped in a kind of hushed mutual pity. When he looks at me I cannot tell what he is seeing. But the change in him is stark. His expression used to be fleshed and vague, all its features swimming into one another. Now they have withdrawn beneath the lantern of his forehead, yet are individually in sharper focus – the nose and jaw-line exposed and delicate. His moustache is a grey stain. He starts to ask what happened to me: but I can only reply one-dimensionally. It seems instead that the answers to myself must be locked up in him, somewhere behind that old elusiveness and pre-occupation, his murmuring tones.

He asks: 'You don't know how long you've been like this?'

'I think only two or three days.'

'Two or three . . . Eddy . . . when is your last memory?' His nervous coughing starts up.

I think of my mother's birthday two years ago, and how he and she planted a eucryphia tree together by the orchard. Nothing later has surfaced in my mind. I can hear the clicking of the collies' feet over the kitchen tiles. My father's hands tense on his knees. For the moment, because nothing has been said, everything seems possible. He can still mention that she is out or ill. And I linger like a coward just this side of knowing, and so keep her here, in possibility, a second longer. Then I hear myself say softly: 'I remember mama's sixty-second birthday.'

He lets out a tiny 'Ah!' and then 'Aah'.

I feel I've committed suicide. When I at last look at him, I see all his evasiveness running wild, his eyes swimming like fish behind their glasses. At last he says: 'Let's walk in the garden, Eddy.' It is his solicitousness, the muted compassion, which is so unnerving.

We go out between the yew hedges along the border to the sundial. An early butterfly has settled there. My father's steps begin to drag and falter. Then he stops, not looking at me, and says at last: 'You know she died, don't you?'

I wait for the words to detonate inside me. Staring at the grass. They set up a slow, hopeless reverberation. I say: 'Yes.'

I sense his relief. I struggle mentally to understand what the words convey – that I will never see her again. The word *never* throbs inside my head. But instead of sudden anguish I feel an ache of desolation, and I realise that at some inaccessible level of myself, yes, I did know, and that I have already suffered and been remoulded by this, so that while my brain receives her death with bitter shock, I am in fact already steeped in it.

And now he is walking again in precise, hesitant steps over the grass, and I notice that his brogues are unpolished, and hear the breathy sound of my own voice: 'How did she die?'

He leaves a tiny pause of disbelief at my blankness. Then he says: 'She had cancer of the liver. It was inoperable. She went very quickly. A year and three months ago.'

'Did she have much pain?'

'Yes, some. But they drug them now, you know.'

My whisper continues: 'Was I with her?' I feel I must be talking of someone else.

'Oh yes, Eddy. In the last week we were with her all the time. Aunt Anna came down from Scotland, and we took turns by her bed. You, me, Anna, through the night. I've never seen Anna like that. She just sat there. She hardly spoke. Mama kept patting her hand, trying to comfort her.' We are walking along the edge of the orchard. He glances at me sometimes, out of his settled sadness, to see how I'm reacting. 'Even at the end I never thought she'd die. You know how she always overcame things.'

'Yes.' But I cannot really grasp this. Everything seems static, embalmed in past time; only I am swimming in it. I feel as if he's talking about the future. And there is something shocking about the rush of his revelation. I've never heard him divulge so much. All my life I've wanted him to unwrap himself, and now that he is doing so I feel apprehensive. He no longer seems my father, and I want him to return.

He goes on: 'But you were splendid, Eddy. She'd got very light, and when the nurse wasn't there you'd carry her to the bathroom in your arms, she complaining of course. You seemed to be willing life into her. You've always had a great optimism, Eddy, like her.'

'Did I?' I don't recognise this. I think I just loved possibility, and had naked ambition.

'Yes, you were . . . strong together . . . you and she. You were willing her to recover, I know, telling her body to match her spirit, as it were.'

He sounds wan and faintly wistful. Her death has eroded but not broken him. It is already a little way away. I long for my own memories to overtake his. I cannot imagine this person lifting up my mother. But my father's recollections are all that is left, the only truth. I even experience the fear that they have usurped the space where mine might have returned, and have obliterated them.

We reach the fringe of orchard by the eucryphia tree, which stands no higher than two years ago: a sliver of dull green. Involuntarily I stop beside it, as if remembrance might gather strength here and roll forward. Perhaps my father understands. He hovers delicately, not looking at the tree. I remember him beside my mother, standing it at her feet where she planned to plant it. It was she, of course, who shouldered the spade and dug it in, and now she reappears in smarting detail: a stout, rose-cheeked woman with bouncing hair and blue

33

eyes, uncaring of appearances. I recall her tossing the turf behind her and bedding in the tree with fertiliser, patting the earth as she would a puppy. 'There now! Grow!' My father had explained that it would put out clusters of creamy flowers in ten years, or so the nursery had said, then added whimsically: 'When you're old you can take tea under it.'

'Whisky,' said my mother. He touched her shoulder in quick, inhibited affection, and gave his dry laugh. She said: 'And what makes you think you won't be here as well, drinking tea?'

My father wore his curious, beaten look. 'Women last longer.'

She scowled comically. 'We'll watch it bloom together!' And the cancer already eating her.

All through their marriage, for as long as I can remember, my mother grew stouter while my father dwindled. She was the daughter of a west country landowner, and even after my father became headmaster of a reputable private school, the notion that she had 'married beneath her' would spatter his talk from time to time. But he was adept at self-deprecation. From photographs I see that a bruised look slowly settled over him, I don't know why. All my childhood I remember him preoccupied, as if he'd just mislaid something. My mother, meanwhile, poured herself into whatever grew and responded: her family, her garden, breeding the perfect collie. She and my father were happy in their way. They continued fruitfully to bemuse one another. He admired her energies. She looked after him like a second child. They made each other important.

Some moment of intuitive sadness, I think, intruded on the scene by the eucryphia, or I wouldn't remember. But even in my mother's jutting chin and blue eyes I sensed a fleeting awkwardness. For five seconds they gazed at it together in odd silence. They did not care that it would outlive them both, I think, only that it would still be blooming when one was there and the other not.

When I try to recover semblances of her – snapshots as from a mental album – they are bewilderingly few. It is as if my visual retention slackens with familiarity, so that the more loved and accepted the face the fewer, or less distinct, are the images I keep of it. Does this spring from amnesia? I don't know. It's like a desertion. Even her precise features are not quite immediate to me. I have to think about them.

My father's footsteps on the lawn beside me, tentative, make me wonder how he too will fade in my memory. Furtively I note the mottled curve of his forehead, the blue-veined hands, so that I will keep them alive.

As if to close the subject of my mother, he half turns to me and says: 'Eddy, we'll carry on together.' But he must know that he is abrogating to himself a power of consolation which he does not have – nor I for him. I think then how precious he is to me – but how much less than she was. He is looking at the ground.

Once or twice I assemble composite portraits which are anchored in the places were she sat or stood. But it is the other ones – the vivid, inexplicable images – which I crave. And now out of my memory I am striding beside her along a lane nearby, while she trots the collies on its tarmac to strengthen their pasterns. It is one of those recollections which arrive, as peripheral friends arrive in dreams, for no reason you can guess. But the unimportance of it – her quietly jubilant smile ('Making the best collie in the world!'), and the concentration in her round eyes and the way she yanks up the leads – 'Heads up! Up!' – merges it with the texture of every day, deepening its value. 'Look at this one! No damn class!' She pulls it up short. 'Where's your deportment? I haven't the patience for you!'

My father lets out a little sigh. 'I'm worried about you, Eddy . . . .' My mother's death is old to him; but mine – my mental death – is new, and sometimes I catch him looking at me with appalled bewilderment. 'The doctor who rang said you'd just walked out of the hospital. So I made an appointment for you in London. I don't know if this was right.'

'Yes . . . yes, it was.' Twenty-four hours now, and I feel no movement in my head. 'I can't explain it. I don't understand.' Instead I want him to explain. I only feel I've aged wretchedly, more than the two years of my memory loss. I stare at him. 'Why would it happen?'

'Why? I don't know.' His hands clasp each other. 'Sometimes people get struck on the head . . . .'

'The doctor couldn't find any injury. He implied it was due to stress, to things happening.'

'Well, a proper examination should establish that . . . I would think . . . . It's best not to worry.' He's pausing and coughing again: the father of my childhood. Whatever he had found a while ago, he's mislaid again.

We are still walking in the ghost of her garden, where the shapes and colours are waiting in shoots and buds. I see where plants have spread uncontrolled, and others shrunk in their shadow. A garden, my mother used to say, is so fragile. I wish she were here to explain me. She'd have ordered up the memories like puddings. But somewhere, I feel, even if he shrinks from it, my father has access to me too. He is not stupid or insensitive. I stop suddenly, forcing him to turn. I say almost angrily: 'Father, tell me what you think.'

He wears his aggrieved look. 'You were ill, yes, rather . . . .'

'What sort of ill?'

'Well, I haven't seen much of you this past year . . . but you were stressed, I should say. You stopped being yourself.'

'What happened? Was it Mama?' But I had thought myself weaned from home.

'That may have started it. I don't know. But you were stronger than the rest of us then.'

We walk on for a moment. My father's voice comes strained and thin: 'You were always a difficult mixture, you know.' He makes me sound like a cake. 'Tough in some ways, very determined . . . .' He stops.

I wait for him to continue, but he doesn't. I mumble a frequent passage from my school reports: ' "Sanders is arrogant and self-willed." '

He laughs, remembering. 'But you were always too sensitive for your own good, Eddy. Some things you took too hard.' What is he not telling me? Doesn't everyone think they're sensitive? 'It's better not to push memories. Let them come. Don't torture yourself. Maybe they'll come when you're ready.'

'I'm ready now.' I sound bitter.

His hands flutter and subside. 'Just . . . give it

time.'

But his evasiveness begins to alarm me. It's like boxing with mist. I feel erupting in me the morbid and indefinable fear that I have done something. I cannot imagine what it is. I try to guess some crime I might commit, out of selfish drive or temper. Then I stare into his face and ask outright: 'Did I do something?'

He looks baffled. 'What sort of thing?'

'Some crime, some accident?' I try to pin his eyes with mine. At last I say: 'Have I killed someone?'

'Of course not, of course not.' I have the odd feeling that he is comforting himself. 'You haven't done anything.' He shakes his head. 'Nothing.'

'Why should I need to forget, then?'

'We all need to forget things.' He takes off his glasses to polish them. Perhaps he doesn't want to see. 'Sometimes one just gets tired.'

'You don't get amnesia because you're tired.'

'No.'

But I feel a vague relief, squeeze his arm. Perhaps only my imagination turns me guilty. It is just a feeling. Guilt without deed, without reason.

We start back towards the house. My father has gone silent. We pass the ornamental pool, where the clogged roots of lilies lie under auburn water. A faint circle in the grass marks where in my boyhood he assembled our home-made observatory, complete with a Newtonian reflector telescope. On starlit nights I would crouch beside him while he scrutinised Norton's Star Atlas and slanted the silver tube skyward. To me he became a sorcerer. Years later, in adulthood, I thrilled to the Giotto satellite's pictures of Halley's Comet and the scanning of Uranus and Neptune by Voyager 2.

But nothing ever equalled the night when my father set my nine-year-old eye to our garden telescope and I saw, hanging in the dark, the yellow orb of Saturn, swept by its ring of gold. On other nights we followed the phases of Venus and glimpsed the polar ice-caps on Mars. The daylight world dwindled away. Always my father would locate the planet or the constellation first, then touch my shoulder and say: 'Look now.' And I would see, suspended in silence as if he had conjured it, the cosmic dust of a nebula unimaginably far, or a planet turning in silence like a golden coin. For nine days, every night, we watched the planetary moons emerge as points of light behind Jupiter, and saw their shadows travel eerily across its belted surface.

Nobody else, not even my mother, comprehended this passion. At school I kept it to myself. The stars belonged to my father and me. Beneath them we were awed into whispering, as if we might frighten them away. 'There's Andromeda . . . . Look . . . . And that's Cassiopeia . . . .' Sometimes his hand would alight on my wrist or arm – the only times he ever touched me – and he would say startling things: that beyond our own galaxy lay an estimated hundred thousand million more, some measuring hundreds of thousands of light years across . . . . But gradually, after we had returned indoors, this intimacy would dissipate, and he would withdraw into his day-to-day self, leaving me still elated with the skies, but feeling obscurely deserted, confused by the shedding of his wizard's cloak.

As we pass the shadowy circle (the telescope was sold to neighbours years ago), I remember the night my mother came out and joined us, kneeling in the grass beside him and peering impatiently through the ocular while he turned it on the planets one by one. The memory is old, but still stark in its precision – a lapis bracelet tinkles on her wrist – so that for a moment I dread the return of images singly out of amnesia (if that is what may happen) because with each one I may mourn her anew. She addressed my father as though the night skies were all his doing. 'Could there be life on that one?' she demanded. 'No? What about *that* one then? Still no?' She nudged him to resight. 'Now, how about that bright yellow one? Still no life?' And after a while she lost interest, and teased him – 'What a waste of space!' – and put on her rural Devon accent, in which she would impersonate a village idiot: 'Don't 'ee go interferin' with God's works, Mister Sanders. Just let the little boggers shine . . . .'

By now we have climbed the terrace to the house, and my father is fumbling with the kitchen door, where the sound of my voice has set the collies scratching and whining. The next moment they are thrusting their wet noses into my hands. The muzzle of the oldest has turned quite white, and her body thickened. The youngest I do not recognise at all. My father fondles them as he never did when my mother was alive, and turns to brew up coffee in a little percolator. He asks: 'Will you be going back to an empty house?'

'Naomi will be there.'

He says vaguely: 'All the same . . . .' He finds a scoop and brushes a few crumbs from the draining-board. His natural fastidiousness has increased.

I hear myself say: 'I know this will seem strange, father, but who is Naomi?'

He winces in disbelief. At the moment my

oblivion is harder for him than for me. 'Don't you remember *anything* about her?'

I think I remember the ghost of a face, and of course her impact. Something haunting and disruptive, I can't explain. I say: 'I only know she evoked . . . . I'm not even sure what. Perhaps it was just falling in love.' I'm sounding like a schoolboy. 'But who exactly is she?'

My father watches me over the rim of his coffee-cup. I think he is pitying me. 'She's an artist, rather good I believe. The daughter of a circuit judge, your mother's class of people' – the little wince again – 'but your mother never met her.'

'How long have I known her?' This is sounding grotesque.

'About a year I think, Eddy . . . yes, that's right . . . . She was a friend of some colleague at the observatory. Then you moved in with her quite suddenly, or so it seemed to me . . . four months ago. You only brought her here twice.'

'Did you like her?'

His eyes start their wandering. He never answers anything directly. 'I'm not sure I quite understood her. At first I thought her rather a weak character – but soon I changed my mind.'

'Why?'

'Well, nothing precise, you know, just the way a person is . . . .' He's turning her as elusive as himself.

'What else?'

'Well, she's slim, nice-looking.' He sounds like a dating agency now. 'Intellectual, I think, and quiet, a bit delicate perhaps, I don't know. I suspect she's not easy. Artist's temperament and all that. But she listens. She pays you attention.' The

41

virtues a schoolmaster loves, of course; I think back to the intensity of her portraits and imagine he is right.

'So you did like her in the end?'

'Yes, Eddy. I think you should hold onto her.' He's earnest now. 'Don't let her go.' His coughing starts up. 'I had the impression you certainly . . . loved one another. Did she leave you a telephone number? Do you know where she is?'

'Yes.' I fumble for her note in my wallet. I've been afraid to ring her.

'Perhaps you should let me phone her later . . . warn her . . . .'

His hand hovers out and takes the note from me.

It's hopeless. She shimmers in and out of my mind as four or five different people created by my own fear or wish-fulfilment. I can no longer even picture her. Only she's left behind this charge of yearning and elation and distress. Madness must be like this. I'm longing to see her, but I don't know who it is I'm longing to see. These aches – guilt, loss, longing – just hammer on alone. They no longer have any object or cause. I love some-one I've forgotten.

5

Over forty hours now, and still, nothing. My return to her cottage and the empty night made no change, but now it is morning – a grey slab of sky – and by afternoon she will be back. I go out to the headland where we must often have walked, and along the cliff path. I receive no sense that I have ever been here before. Far out to its blurred horizon the sea is a plain of grey. At every twist of the path a realigned view of promontories and inlets promises that one of them will strike a memory. Beneath me, for three hundred feet, the cliffs drop sheer, fissured horizontally as if shaken loose by wind. Whole segments have detached themselves and crashed into the waves, where the water curdles white and icy turquoise against their debris.

I try to imagine her beside me, and sometimes I think I do, but she's always just out of focus, and has no special tone of voice and no thoughts. She just is. I can't resurrect her more. Under the blonde-streaked hair (and I'm not sure of that now) the oval of her face encloses nothing. Her features have been airbrushed out. The fact that I'll see her within a few hours scarcely mitigates this pain. What can this unremembered person be to me? How do I love her? It is the woman subtle with the past whom I want to retrieve. At each spur of cliffs the knowledge that we must have stood here gazing along the coast is unbearable. Sometimes I can tell the exact spot where we must have stopped: here where the cliffs bulge in ivy-blackened declivities filled with linnets; farther on by the headland where boulders tilt like stone idols among the flowering sea-cabbage; there where the scarps curve in white palisades crying with gulls, and cormorants are drying their outspread wings on the rocks below.

The ruins of a wartime radar research station scatter a ledge above the tide. The walls have collapsed inwards all of a piece in slabs of cemented bricks, and over their remains and over the cliffs behind them pours a great swathe of vegetation. I clamber down, hoping that something will spur recognition. In the choked doorways, which lead to nothing, old hausers coil indestructibly, and tangles of rusted wire cover the cliffside like bracken. I think: surely I remember this. It's not like anywhere else I've been. It must evoke something. I try to imagine her walking here, saying things. What is she saying? What is she thinking? But my desire only turns the place starker, more actual, and her absence seems to reinforce its repudiating solidity. Once the wind comes and fills its ruins with an ivy-glistening tremor of life.

I throw back the hood of my anorak to meet the wind, let it clean my head out. A clouded sun has emerged to lay a faint, steely glitter on the sea. Behind me the promontory of Portland Bill is creamed in fog, and far in front a lighthouse flashes through the mist. The wind stiffens. I have an idea that it will dissipate something, batter me into memory. It smarts my eyes, buffets my ears. From the chasm below my path, seagulls lift level with me. Then I sit down in the grass. I stop gazing along the coastline, and think: she is an artist, maybe she drew my attention to minutiae. I stare at the quartz-like seams in the limestone, the mauve and mahogany whorls of snails sucking on wood fallen near my arm. Nothing.

Are there tricks for retrieving memory? Maybe the intrusion of something ephemeral is the secret – that distant freighter with its blunt prow and squat funnel, or the army patrol vessel from Lulworth; or perhaps once we heard the churring of the scarlet lobster-boat with its orange floats bunched aft, and cried 'Oh look!', and smiled at the cloud of gulls following it.

But slowly, tramping on, I stop expecting. I watch the daisies and buttercups, newly out, which colour the short grass. If I don't strain, I think, if I simply let my mind rest, perhaps recollection will move into the empty space.

I reach the amphitheatre of a long-disused quarry. Beside it the sea booms in a cove of flattened rocks. Gingerly I enter the vast, level pit. The openings to its galleries still gape in the discoloured scarps. Inside, piers of living rock uphold the gouged emptiness. My feet echo over the tamped earth. Futilely, I call out: 'Naomi!' Somewhere, invisibly, water is dripping. Again I listen for her thoughts. Is she fascinated, bored, a little frightened? 'Naomi!' It's a soft, unechoing name. (Is she Jewish?) Graffiti scatter the walls, scratched by knives or daubed with campers' charcoal. I wonder if, in a playful moment, we might have incised our own. In the shadow I make out 'Lucy, 1995 ... Graham loves Holly ... 1991 Simon + Heather ....'

Just once, on the way back, I experience a

moment of fragility, something elusive, inexplicable. As I pass the empty coastguard station, the slack ropes of its lowered flag are striking the iron flagpole with a thin, repeated *fluk-fluk-fluk* in the wind. In the instant before I realise the source of this sound, I feel that it is dinning in my head from somewhere else, with a different meaning. But the next moment I have located the noise, and its strangeness is gone.

When I get back to the house it is already past noon. I'm unable to eat. I stalk from room to room, looking for I don't know what. I've already rifled through her effects, looked at her photographs (but none of her, I know) and guiltily sifted her correspondence, but found nothing of my own. It's as if I've expunged all my recent life. In the bedroom I pat down my hair in the mirror, put on a new pullover. Sometimes an odd euphoria comes over me, but it's followed by fear. I don't know where to go, so I stand by the window and calm myself by looking at the trees. The blackthorn is out, and I glimpse the dip of swallows under the birches.

Just after three a small blue Peugeot appears in the drive. I pull back and turn away. In the mirror beside me my features look frozen and old. When I slap my cheeks, the colour ebbs. I try to smile at myself, but my face splits emptily in two. This is petrifying, wonderful. I can't imagine setting eyes on her and my memories not flooding back. A car door slams shut. I calm my breathing into a deeper, slower rhythm. From outside comes the click of steps over the path. They stop a few yards from the door.

I wait. Nothing. I move towards it. My heart is crashing. In my mind's eye, in the void of her face under the highlit hair, I suddenly see clear features and slanted eyes. My hand trembles at the latch. I want to open it before she does. I hear nothing on the far side, then pull it back.

Facing me, five yards from the porch, stands a dark girl in shapeless clothes. In one hand she carries a portfolio, in the other an overnight case. She is a complete stranger.

We stare at one another. She is looking straight at me, not speaking. I ask stupidly: 'Naomi?' Then I'm blushing with embarrassment, as if I've committed a social gaffe.

She doesn't move, but says 'Edward'. It's a frightening sound, watchful, trembling. It hesitates just outside familiarity. It remains in the silence a long time. Its last syllable lifts to a questioning whisper, which is trying to reach me, to call back whoever it was she knew.

I look at her with (I know) appalled numbness. I can't help myself. She reminds me of nobody at all. She might have wandered in to ask the way. Her voice stirs nothing. She looks quite plain, apart from her dark eyes.

I hear my own voice, bleak. 'I'm sorry.'

I don't know how long we go on staring at each other. I see on her face the same disbelief as I saw on my father's: but deeper hurt, and touched by a kind of awed pity. At last she says: 'May I come in?', as if the house belongs to me now. I stand aside and she goes past me into the kitchen, laying her portfolio on a chair. She turns, and her stare, in the instant before she composes herself, seems to be sweating with a kind of fear. I think she wants to take me in her arms – or bury herself there – but she doesn't. She stands a little away and just says: 'Your father told me.'

I reply meaninglessly: 'Good.' I don't know what to do. I sit down on the edge of a chair.

She says: 'Have you eaten?' She moves automatically to the fridge. The comfort of habit. 'What would you like?'

'Anything.' I'm staring at her back, trying to make sense of her. I cannot imagine how I came to live here, or ever touching her. I long only to leave.

But I'm ashamed when it is she, very lightly, who comes up and touches my hand and says: 'You mustn't worry. Your mind must have wanted this. Peace. It'll be a turning-point.' Then she sits down a little apart from me. Her skin looks deathly pale against her dark hair, but this may be natural to her. She says: 'Will you tell me what happened?'

'I don't know. I expect I know less than you do.' The words sound helpless. 'I just "came to" the day before yesterday, in this restaurant practically in Gloucester. Two years wiped out. The doctor said I might have been wandering about for days, I've no idea.' I ask: 'When did I leave here? Can you remember?', as if she too might have forgotten.

'Four days ago. You must have been two nights away.' She is watching me now with solemn attentiveness: the kind I imagine she gives to her sitters. She says: 'I should never have let you go.'

'Why did I go?'

'You wanted to be alone.'

'Why?' I don't understand this man who lives in other people's eyes.

'You hadn't been well. You had a lot to cope with.'

'In my work, you mean?'

'In everything.'

48

'How?' She seems to be evading me, just as my father did. 'Did I have some kind of breakdown?'

'Yes, in a way, you did.' She's looking at me quite steadily. It's my eyes, for some reason, which drop from hers. 'But I didn't understand it. Not well enough. You cut yourself off. You became sad, almost desperate. Perhaps I was too anxious not to intrude on you . . . to increase your trouble. And your doctors didn't do well by you.'

'Was I under analysis?'

'No.' She gives a sudden, quick laugh. 'You said you thought psychoanalysis would go down as the failed religion of the twentieth century.'

'Did you agree with me?'

'Yes.' She smiles at me. 'But we probably expect too much.'

Her familiarity with me is unnerving. Instinctively she knows how to speak with me, and already our conversation is settling into the rhythms of couples who have known one another long or intensely. But my only feeling is of continuous, faint surprise. It's not unpleasant. I try to summon a little tenderness for her: 'I'm sure you were good to me . . . . How long have we been together?'

Her voice cools, as if she senses, and repudiates, this condescension. 'We've known each other a year. You came to live here five months ago.'

'I must have been hell to live with.'

'Well, yes!' She laughs.

'Perhaps you precipitated it!' I'm taking refuge in banter. 'It's all your doing!'

'Perhaps. I expect hell is a collusion.'

Yet I wonder what I've really been like, what facets of myself she's known. I've broken into fragments. I exist only as other people's versions. I say: 'All the same, was I good to you?' I'm meaning, I think: did I really love you?

She understands. 'Yes.'

In the silence she gets up and starts to make a salad on the sideboard, slicing cucumber and peppers with flickers of a blunt knife. Covertly I watch her gestures, her way of moving – economical, delicate, tense (but that's because of us) – and wonder what I attached to these before, whether they were charged with some obscure beauty, in what way they moved me. It's unimaginable. I wonder vaguely what she's like in bed. I understand how she confused my father. She's self-contained, cold I daresay. She doesn't care much about her appearance: no make-up, hair tied back in an elastic band. She has an irritating way of brushing back imaginary strands from her face.

I get up to help her, and the drudgery eases us. When she says 'Here are some onions' or 'Try garlic', the words might be prescribing a mutual medicine. She finds Edam cheese and some fresh orange juice (unsettling how she knows what I like) and we take our seats again, as if they too were prescribed. She must know hundreds of things about me – my preferences, opinions, eccentricities – while I know nothing at all about her, and don't much want to.

I hear myself say: 'Perhaps if I regain my memory, I'll go back to Hell.'

'No.' Her palm brushes my hand. 'It'll be like starting again.'

'Do I need to start again? Has my work suffered?'

'No, not your work. Just you.' I'm relieved she doesn't say 'us'.

Grotesque, once or twice, the way she looks at me – lovingly – but I can tell she knows this too, and checks it back. I say almost belligerently: 'You must know why this happened to me.'

'You were suffering in ways I didn't sense.'

'You did sense them. I saw your portraits of me.'

She looks disconcerted. 'Even with someone you love' – but she passes the word quickly, lightly – 'you paint what you see.'

I say angrily: '*You* don't. You paint what you *know*.' I'm thinking: why can't she be open with me? I'm being treated like a patient, a child.

'It doesn't really work like that.' Suddenly she's crouched in front of me. 'Edward, very soon your memories will all start to come back. But you won't retrieve them by hearing facts. I spoke to a specialist this morning. An amnesiac memory can't be jogged by somebody else. It must return from within.' She stands up again. 'You ought to rest now. You're not yourself.'

'I don't believe in a self. Whatever I am now is me.' So she won't explain anything either. This will drive me mad.

'You're trembling, Edward.'

My name sounds foreign on her lips. I don't want it there. 'I'm not trembling.' This is impossible. I say: 'You know, Naomi, there's another girl. There always has been.'

'There were several before. I've only known you a year.'

'There is another now. I'm sorry. There still is.' Her face alters. Suddenly, despite this oblivion, I feel as if I recognise its small, subterranean changes out of past closeness. And this one is a frightened sadness. 'I'm sorry.' I stand up and go to the window. 'Maybe she was with me before

51

you. Amnesia usually shrinks, you know. From the distant past, forward.' I half look round at her, glimpse her shape facing me. I feel suddenly: is this all there is? Nothing here. Only this enormous absence. The memories all wrong here. Some pressure is building inside me, I can't describe. It's taut and close and won't subside. Maybe it's memory trying to come back, and can't. The pulsing has started in my forehead again. I say: 'I'm going off for a few days. I need to be alone.'

'Where?'

I rummage through my mind, remember the letter. 'To an Anglican friary. Yes, there are such things. A friend of mine's a postulant there. Don't worry. I won't black out again.'

Yes, I'll go. I can't stand this otherwise. I'm in the wrong place, hopelessly wrong. I don't know where is right; but not here, not here. The life has gone out of everything here, if it ever had any. Somehow I've got displaced. I write names in my breath on the window-pane, try them out, 'Susie ... Glenda ... Claudia ...' Is any of them her? God knows. Why the hell does my forehead throb like this?

Naomi says: 'Are you all right?'

Yes, I am all right. But I can't stay. I can't wake up every morning to an unknown face. She bears no relation to you whom I love. She doesn't mean a thing to me. I swear I never touched her. She's too pale, too solemn. Christ knows how I came to be here at all. I wipe off the names. Maybe I'm trembling because I'm going to recover you. Yes, tonight, or tomorrow: it's been too long. I'll fill out your face. Let's be happy again, if that is what we were. (Were we?) What more is there?

'Edward ....'

Don't call me that. I don't know you. But I say:
'A day or two. That's all. I won't be long.'

6

I drive west over the twilit hills, and feel a new lightness, new hope. I go past farms already putting themselves to sleep, towns where the shops are closing. The world is simplifying itself. The hubbub in me is dying down. Sometimes it seems to bring me to the brink of remembrance, but this is always illusion. Now I wonder: does it matter? The thought comes: why not another day without memory? A day in the present! I always undervalued the present! A soft, limpid but quite ordinary light has grown on the hills, and the sky is swarming with cauliflower clouds, and the first swallows are here. And this may happen any dusk!

I wonder what an Anglican friary is like. It doesn't sound serious. Perhaps that's why my friend (who was never serious) has taken to it. I imagine a conclave of Friar Tucks, drunk on plainsong and port. Why did he do it? At university there were intense, secular men who might have reverted to Christ through philanthropy or intellectual juggling. But not Harry. He was the cliché undergraduate, swilling beer and always sporting a new girl. He was jolly, forthright, not very clever. I last remember him failing exams on the stock exchange. I wonder fancifully: has he lost his memory and forgotten who he was?

I stop near the centre of Dorchester, wanting to

buy him a bottle of Scotch. He cannot have changed so much that he'd refuse that. I buy this with a bank card and am relieved that it isn't rejected. I've no idea how much money I have. Outside, a light rain is starting to fall. I walk back along lit streets, where late shoppers and clerical staff are still huddled at bus-stops. Casually I scan the illumined restaurants and shop-fronts. On the opposite side a middle-aged woman is undressing mannequins in a couturier's window, and two men are debating something across a bistro table. Looking at the darkening sky, I take refuge under a café awning to wait until the shower passes. Then I turn without thought, and my blood runs cold. Three feet from me a young woman is seated in the café window. It is her.

She is reading a magazine and has not seen me. She does not look up, although my stare floods her. I walk back fast up the street, trying to regain control. My breath comes harsh. I imagine my face dead white. The rain is falling heavily now, plastering my hair. With my face half averted, I go back on the far side. She is still reading. I can see the dyed lights in the hair of her bent head. She is wearing a short black skirt. Above the high, familiar cheekbones I can deduce her eyes from the curl of their lashes: tilted almonds, pearl-grey.

I watch her from the far pavement, the rain pouring down. She lifts a cup to her lips. I feel slightly sick. Euphoria and terror, there's no difference. But in a minute she may go.

I don't remember crossing the street, pushing the door. Now I'm facing her above the table. I must look like a tramp (but it's too late) with my whisky in a bag and my hair straggling. The café is almost empty but I gesture to the seat opposite her. My throat is dry. My voice grates. 'May I join you?'

She looks up beneath her lashes, and smiles. She is very young. I catch a tart whiff of scent. 'Yeah, sure.'

I drop into the chair, light with elation, fear. I say: 'I thought I recognised you.'

Her laugh flutters. 'I've heard that one before.'

But my eyes incinerate her. I pore over every inch of her. I long to take her hands. 'Don't you remember me? You must. It can't be so long ago.'

'Where'd we meet then?' She frowns. 'We didn't meet at Lindy's?'

'I can't remember where. I just know we did.' Surely you must recognise me. You can't just look bemused, sip that coffee. 'We know each other. Don't we know each other?'

She laughs again, pertly. 'Well, we do now.'

'No, I promise you, we met in some other time. If you . . . .'

'You mean, in another life?' She's interested now. Tentatively she holds out the pendant on her necklace. 'This is the Hindu mantra, you know, my Om.' She lets me touch it. 'Do you really think we've met? D'you believe in transmigration? Maybe we knew each other in another incarnation, and that's why you recognise me.'

'You think?' I wonder wildly if this could be true. I'm drinking in the contours of her face, her neck, her legs beneath the too-tight skirt. Only the timbre of her voice offends what I half-remember: it tinkles. But I'm terrified she'll get up and go. A sliver of carrot cake still lies on her plate, but her coffee is drained. 'I don't know about other lives. But perhaps you're right. There has to be some explanation.'

56

'It all depends on your chakras. I think you're more air, and I'm more earth. I can usually sense these things.' Her mouth is wide, turns up at the corners. 'That means you're higher, but in my next life I may ascend to you . . . .' She lifts her hand. It's fine and slender, as I expected, but on all but the marriage finger glint cheap rings. I ache to hold it. 'But sometimes your energies can go wrong.'

'How?'

'Well, we've all got this kundalini inside us, I mean, this snake . . . no, not a real snake, stupid . . . a kind of mystic thing, which gives you energy, sex and that. D'you know?'

I don't know anything. I just long to kiss you, take you against me. I don't know why you frighten me. It's easy, after all, kissing. It's holding that's the problem. People slip away. I say: 'No, I don't mean any mysticism . . . I mean I lost you in my memory . . . I don't even know your name.'

'Sandra. What's yours?'

I sieve back my damp hair in my fingers. I know this is ridiculous, but if I've lost my memory of you, perhaps you've lost yours of me too. So we meet in this café in nowhere (Dorchester, is it?) and talk in words that can't find each other. With Naomi, who recognises me, I feel as distant as Pluto. With you, who don't, I've come home. 'Edward, my name is Edward.' For some reason I add: 'I'm an astronomer.'

'Oh, how fascinating! I said you were an air spirit! And I've always wanted to do astronomy.' Your eyes swim over me. They're like porcelain. 'But I've never believed in the stars. I mean in astrology, and that. They say everything's changed since the Babylonians anyway, isn't that right?

The "houses" all overlap now, or something. But don't the stars make you feel very tiny, like you're hardly there? I know they would me.'

'You get used to it.'

She fondles her mantra and looks at me almost with awe. 'What are you watching up there then?'

I realise I don't know what I'm working on now; I only hope it hasn't changed. But I say: 'Sometimes a live star and a dead star circle one another. That's what I'm studying. You can't see the dead star because it's dark. We call it a black hole. It's collapsed inwards. But the disc around it sends out signals, and I'm monitoring them. Slowly the bright star gets eaten up by the dark one.'

'Do you find a lot of that, then? A light star and a dark one going round one another?' She makes it sound immoral.

'Yes, the skies are probably full of them.' It seems strange, put like that, but black holes may already dominate the universe. Increasing more than the stars. But when I look at the chance molecules which are you, it's irrelevant.

'It sounds rather horrible,' she says.

Momentarily her brightness dims. I seem to have opened up some sadness in her, and I feel irrationally nervous. I want to comfort her. 'It'll be millennia of years before this affects us.' Yes, by the time it matters we will all be gone. We'll have been recycled countless times – transmigrated into atoms – until at last we become pure energy. It doesn't matter. Only I can't bear your brightness dimming.

You say: 'It's all a bit brainy for me.'

I'm feeling faintly sick. I want to take your

hand. Surely some part of you must be sliding back into memory? 'What do you do?'

'I'm a secretary in that solicitor's over the road. But it's not like your job, I mean, it's not clever. I wanted to do marital, that's where it's fun, but I'm stuck in conveyancing.'

A cup of coffee has turned tepid by my hand. I don't even remember ordering it. She's happy again. I ask: 'What's your surname?'

She starts to blush. 'Smith. Isn't that awful? I hate Smith.'

The colour travels along her cheekbones, touches her clear jaw line. She's beautiful. Almost unthinking, I take her hand. Its fingers curl against mine. Their warm pressure is more than I can bear. I say: 'Let's go somewhere.'

'Where d'you want?'

'Anywhere.'

'This town's a dump. We could try a movie but my flat-mate Rosie says they're all lousy this week. There's some horror film on about snakes. But we could go back to our place if you like. There may be something on TV.'

It's round the corner, a four-minute walk. The drizzle has lifted and she skips over puddles, laughing. She has wonderful legs. Now that we're out here, I wonder what I'm doing, and I don't know. Who is she? I just walk beside her. When we enter her flat, and find Rosie out, I feel like a teenager. But my temples are throbbing again. I'm in a room whose walls are plastered with posters of Hindu godlings, Salvador Dali prints, and photos of pop stars. The floor is littered with cassettes. Some joss-sticks and a postcard of a Buddhist guru stand on the mantelshelf.

I say: 'Do you think that's true, that we've lived

other lives?' I want her in my arms.

She's stepped close to me. 'Oh yes, don't you?'

I smell her scent. I know I mustn't touch her. She's not you. She can't be you. She's just an optical illusion, a simulacrum. So why am I shaking? I say: 'I believe it if you do.' Do I? Her face lifts to mine, and becomes inescapable. She dangles me from her eyes. I cup her carved cheekbones in my hands. I'm trembling. For a second I elude her lips. Her breasts push against me, touch me with pain. My sex swells helplessly.

She whispers: 'Careful.'

I've lost my sense of time, so fragile. Now I sink my lips on yours. You stream through me. I'm kissing the dream of you. The oval of your face is filled with features now, just as I knew: straight nose, pearl eyes. And my hands start to remember your body: shoulders, breasts. Everything burns to seal you, pinion you, so you'll never leave me again. My fingers find the zip of your skirt, drop it to your feet, and it's no good your trying to repel me (your hands beating on my shoulders now) because now I enfold you, your thighs smooth under my hands, tights slipping down. Soon I'll elide you into me, stick you to me with the glue of my love, my will, and you'll never get away again, never embitter, or pull back or mock . . . .

'Stop!' Her face has jerked back from mine, staring. My eyes are streaming tears. 'I didn't mean I'd do that!'

I hear my voice pleading. '*Please. Stay.*' Then a bitterness erupts in me from nowhere I know, and I'm shouting. 'Why is it always like this?'

She breaks from me. 'Why is what always like what?'

'Why do you always destroy everything?'

60

'I don't know what you're talking about. You don't even know me!'

'I *do*.'

But her face shows only stunned innocence. I see us suddenly as ridiculous. She's standing in front of me, her skirt forgotten, primping her hair. Her legs end in a pair of green high-heels. There's a patch of semen spreading over my trousers. She says: 'I didn't think you'd be that way. All your talk of recognising me, and that.'

'I did. I do.' I feel dazed.

'Why are you crying?' She pulls on her skirt. 'I don't understand you, I really don't. Men.' She sighs, anticipating years of bafflement. But she doesn't move from where she's been standing. She's calm now, calmer than I am, and turns and says rather formally: 'Look. Maybe I gave you the wrong idea. I may not be very bright, but I'm not a one-night stand.' She runs her hands over her breast, reaffirming herself, then leaves her fingers spread there, as if she's forgotten them, long and fine, covered in their sullying rings.

I can't explain the depths to which I've used her. When I say 'I'm sorry', the sound cracks and sighs. Because a chaotic guilt is erupting in me, as if I'd raped her. The fantastical idea occurs that I hurt her even before we met, and that she's punishing me. I say: 'I don't know what's happening to me.'

'Maybe you should see someone.' She's pulling up her tights. 'My friend Rosie goes to a counsellor on Fridays. Or you could try meditation. I know it sounds funny, but I do meditation.'

Even as she's zipping up her skirt, adjusting her cuffs, the mystery of her body returns, and I long to kiss her again. Yet I wonder, had she slept with me, what would have been beyond. And I sense a great coldness: not hers, but the dying of illusion, which is all there is.

Suddenly she says: 'Oh God.'

'What?'

'One of my earrings is bust. They cost seventeen quid.'

The next moment she's on the floor, hunting for it, and I've joined her, and we're starting to laugh.

By the time I reach the friary it is almost midnight, and a caretaker leads me tiredly to the guest-wing. Across the courtyard the chapel windows smoulder with a dim light, and muffled chanting rises. But I fall asleep still dressed on the hard bed, and wake with the morning pouring through a window whose curtains I never closed.

I lie listening to unaccustomed sounds: lambs bleating on the slopes, the trill of swallows, silence, and at last the high *ding-ding-ding* of the bell for morning prayer. I walk out over grass flecked with fallen blossom. The friary is squat and down-to-earth: a quadrangle of rustic buildings drawn round a garden court. But a dewy light turns the circling hills into the backdrop to a painting.

I slip into the rear of the chapel. Some thirty people – monks and laymen – crowd the pews or sit on benches lining the walls. It is very simple. Candles glimmer beneath an icon, a carved saint. A bare cross hangs behind the bare altar. The chanting and antiphonal prayers fill the space with a hushed collusion. The monks, smudged out of worldly scale by their brown robes, might have migrated out of Chaucer. There are hoary elders with dishevelled white locks and icicle beards; a pair of acolytes with eager, discordant voices; slight, balding saints whose pates glimmer like collapsed haloes. Amongst them I notice a big, hirsute man who booms out the canticles and who genuflects and crosses himself more often and emphatically than the others. It is several minutes before I realise, with a shock, that this is Harry.

For a moment I cannot take my eyes from him, as if he had appeared out of context or in a dream. Then I unfocus onto the altar where the crucified Christ hangs painlessly in incense, and find my lips forming the responses. It is years since I believed in them, yet they bring an obscure comfort, as if reintegrating me with my past. (I am frail, I know.) Momentarily their incantation seems to create God in the gloom, feeds me with a dream or a folk memory. I sing them in my head. I try to let them fill me. Yet when I watch the monks in their ritual gestures and perambulations, their uplifted books and half-closed eyes, they inhabit some other stratum than mine, somewhere undisclosed to me, or lost.

> *For behold, you look for truth deep within me,*
> *and will make me to understand wisdom secretly.*
> *Purge me from sin and I shall be pure . . . .*

I push against the walls of my amnesia, as if it were responsible for my exile, for this sense of listening to a mistranslated language. What do they call sin? Sin cuts you off from God. Is that why I feel estranged here? My guilt seems to float untethered, like a Christian leftover, a natural state. It feels heavy and certain. Sometimes it churns my stomach. My father said I'd done nothing wrong, but he never answers questions fully. I should have asked Naomi, and watched her eyes. Guilt: perhaps it comes simply because I've fallen ill. I'm guilty of obliterating everyone over two years, of abdicating responsibility. Of self-forgiveness. I may have committed anything, but my conscience is wiped clear. I've become a monster.

The antiphonal chanting still hums inside me. But my thoughts run wild. Maybe in the past two years I underwent a conversion. Perhaps I'm in a state of grace, but don't know it. If I've lost all memory of my conversion, is it annulled? Am I returned to sin? Or am I unwittingly a believer? This is a conundrum for God.

But Harry has regained his faith, and become a child again. How did it happen? My eyes return to him. He looks big with some unexploded mystery. I cannot make up my mind if he has soared into a prophet or dwindled to a baby. His brown smock displaces him. He looks by turns daunting, un-fathomable, and faintly absurd.

A new heart I will give you,
and put a new spirit within you,
And I will remove from your body the heart of stone
and give you a heart of flesh.

The monks' heads go back in unison, their mouths open. The language they sing, even in the modernised text, celebrates mysteries which I no longer deeply understand: grace, heavenly redemption, the arcane gift of the dead Son. The air is thick with symbols. Blood, wine, cross. They swarm around a truth which slips away. I try to recover it. But this glittering ritual seems to circle only a void of wish-fulfilment, like the accretion disc of a black hole, shining with trapped stars.

When the service ends and we troop out by

65

separate doors, I avoid Harry, I don't know why. I glimpse him filing with other brothers towards the refectory, and I take a different path. He wrote to me as if we hadn't met for years, so there's nothing we've shared which I have forgotten. This should bring a cleansing relief to our talk. But for the moment I walk in the orchards, and wonder who he now is.

The apple and cherry trees are in blossom, and the viburnums float out layers of creamy flowers as if underwater. I trespass into the monks' quarters, cluttered with chapels and oratories. Their doorways are flanked by stoops of holy water, and inset with tiles of doves bearing olive branches with *Pax et Bonum* inscribed above. Ceramic tondos of saints gleam in the walls. The gardens are attended by figures of Virgins with Child, Virgins with flowers, Virgins with lanterns. It is pure, peaceful, childish. At the end of a lime avenue, in a cemetery overlooking the hills, the monks lie buried under slabs inscribed only with their Christian names, as if they had lost – or found – their identity in brotherhood. Beyond them the heads of trees gather like water in the valleys.

Then the refectory bell rings, and I go in to breakfast. It is held in silence. The brothers and guests sit mingled, and I find myself cushioned between a sad-faced silentiary in brown and a sister of St Clare smiling private thoughts. Eventually, from the far end of the table, Harry catches sight of me. For an instant I expect him to look embarrassed, sitting as he is in a russet smock at a linoleum-topped table with a bowl of porridge and monastic rhubarb. But instead his face explodes in grins and he comes over and silently clasps my head in a pair of hands which seem to have become swollen, while the brothers look on indulgently and the nun goes on smiling. Then he returns to his place, and nothing is heard but the slurp of porridge and the crunch of teeth into toast. Furtively I watch the other monks and wonder how he survives – he whose college parties were raucous with champagne and irreverence and sex-play. Yet he shines now with the same inebriate happiness as he did then. He pushes a pot of marmite at the postulant beside him. When he winks at me it is not collusive, just a merry habit. He looks as if he's singing inside. I stare down at my plate and want to understand. I accept a hunk of bread and some coarse marmalade from the monk beside me. We sip weak tea. Our knives and cups clatter in the silence. Harry, I remember, was never an aesthete, just a hedonist. But still I don't understand. The rattle of my tea-cup is the last sound before breakfast ends.

'You fox! I never expected you! When did you get here?' He manhandles me out of the refectory. He's staring at me. 'How long has it been? Five years? Seven? You'll tell me everything! What are you doing? Are you still star-gazing?' He makes it sound a sublime irrelevance. He doesn't wait for my replies. We march through the courtyard and out into the orchards. 'What do you think of this place? Isn't it beautiful?'

I say: 'But what are the monks like?'

'Oh they're a good lot, these. I know they look dull and all alike, sitting mum like that, but in private they're a riot. The little one is a stand-up comic. Brother Terry was a professional footballer, Brother Hugo . . . .'

As he talks on, I remember how he always longed for companionship, the peculiar re-assurance craved by undergraduates seeking a shared soul, like ants or bees. I never understood it. I think I was too arrogant to be part of anything. Even now I hear my own voice, mystified: 'What do you *do* all day?'

'Everything here's kept simple, Eddy. I get up at six-thirty for morning prayer, then work in the vegetable garden and kitchen. Sometimes I serve in the chapel – we have four short services a day – and part of the afternoon and evening goes in bible study and theology with one of the brothers.'

'Does it ever change?' There's a fearful bleak-ness in my question, but he doesn't hear it.

'The monks study less than the postulants. Otherwise, not much change, no. There's a lot of maintenance.' He laughs suddenly, uproariously. 'I've just remembered something you used to say! "I love creating but hate maintaining." Do you re-member saying that?'

'No, but it sounds like me!' I'm laughing too. I touch his arm. The past has grown precious.

'You always were impatient. You seemed to rush about devouring things. You made me feel like a clod!' He kicks a clump of earth. 'And what are you looking for up in space now? Have you found a new form of life?'

'Yes,' I say. 'But down here. You!' We are walk-ing through young bluebells. 'What the hell are you doing? How did this happen?'

I find it unbearable that his life seems over. I can imagine no movement in it, no change, ever. It rolls in my head through a frozen orbit of comfort and decay, in the chapel, the scullery, among the flowering and dying laburnums, talking to his God through the chanting, the silences, from novitiate to death in the cemetery overlooking the hills.

Yet he is swinging his arms, bursting with life. He says: 'I suppose my feelings had been changing for ages, Eddy, long before I realised it. Then one day I came home to find my house burgled. Swept clean! Everything gone! They'd even found the car-key and driven off my Saab.' His words rush and bounce together. I know what is coming, of course, but feel a tinge of wonder. I still imagine I am walking beside an earlier Harry, not this buoyant ascetic. He clasps my shoulder. 'My first instinct was to replace everything, of course. I started making long lists: my videos, CDs, silver, leather . . . . And then – quite suddenly – I realised I had lost all interest in them. I just didn't care. Do you remember that climbing holiday we took in the Pyrenees? Laying out everything we thought we'd need, and then discarding almost all of it? Well, it was like that. I realised I needed nothing. I was just left with myself. Maybe the possessions had helped me become what I am. But in themselves they didn't matter. I was free.'

I feel myself grimace, but he doesn't notice. I haven't confessed my amnesia to him, and I won't now. Because my tragedy is the reverse of his triumph: a blight which preserves possessions, but removes the self. By now we have entered a pinewood split by gullies. Its trees bloom only high above us, like rainforest, leaving aisles of dark trunks and branches, and a dust of needles underfoot. I had expected to approach his conversion delicately, like an illness. But he booms on: 'Then I thought: what's it all about? What's it telling me? Well, if there's any point to existence, I thought, it can only be God. So nothing's more important than serving Him. Nothing! D'you see? D'you see? I thought: look at the beauty of things! Isn't it time to trust? Kierkegaard said that belief was like letting yourself down a well on a rope – the rope of reason – and then trusting to leap into the dark of faith. And that's what I did! And it's light! Light!'

He turns to face me. His postulant's tunic transmutes him to a huge infant. He keeps clasping and unclasping his hands. His eyes bulge and wander astray, a little freakishly. Yet there's something impressive about him, as if he's grown a size bigger. I had thought him unchanged, but I am wrong. Some part of him is out of my reach. I even feel momentarily small beside him, and it irks. Too much of me has been taken away already. He says: 'And I always thought you were the religious one.'

'*Me*?'

'Yes. It was you who used to be hunting after some kind of sense, some meaning. While I spent university enjoying myself!'

'Don't you miss that?' I hesitate. 'Women, for instance?'

But he shrugs. 'To tell you the truth, Eddy, I feel I've got through all that. I used to worship women . . . you remember Sophie, Carla? But after . . . when the mystery goes . . . .' He appears suddenly doltish. I notice the backs of his hands, quite smooth and hairless. 'It's enough for me to love the Lord.' But his face strikes me abruptly as more oiled, more jowly than I remember, as if he were passing gently to a eunuch state.

We walk on over the soundless pine-needles. He thrusts and blunders between the trunks, and the dead branches snap off against his shoulders. He grows boisterous and voluble again. 'Haven't you ever wanted to know the purpose of everything, Eddy? You're an astronomer. You see all that majesty!'

I say: 'Your God is in history, Harry. Astronomy makes history seem small.' My voice sounds tight, arid. 'Of course I'd like to think the Big Bang was triggered for a purpose by some astral patriarch. But purpose is a human concept, and God isn't human, presumably.' I'm surprised at my own bitterness. Perhaps in my amnesiac years I've been engaged in some private dialogue with Him, to no avail.

But Harry is unperturbed. 'How did things start then? How? Can't you believe in a providence that cares?'

I think: now he's as facile as I remember. I try to contain my irritation. I say: 'I've no idea what started things, and nor have you. To suppose it's someone's brain-child is infantile, anthropo-centric. I think it's more honest, more decent, to admit ignorance.'

But Harry only laughs. 'You physics men were always too bright for me.'

'We just try not to invent things.' Yet I feel reduced by him, I don't know why. 'I can't per-sonalise God. I don't think it's relevant to say he cares or doesn't care. In that sense He doesn't exist.'

He shakes his head. 'That's a poor sort of God.'

'I can't create another because it suits me.' Yet he refuses to be insulted. The tension is all in me. My breath comes light, fast. He's dealing in day-dreams. I say hotly: 'You think a perfect God is an explanation for a suffering world?'

'Oh no, I wouldn't say that.' He places a hand on my forearm. He is looking at me with a kind of

71

compassion. To my surprise I don't feel insulted, but a little moved. 'It must be difficult,' he says, 'being you.'

I don't know what he means. After a minute he says: 'You don't seem yourself.'

'Nor do you!'

'But something's shaken you, hasn't it?' He's frowning in puzzlement. 'Is it a woman? Or has someone died?'

Suddenly, stark above us, a life-size Christ is hanging nailed to a beech tree. I stare in mute shock. It is unaccountably sinister. He dangles there in agony, like a suicide. Set up as an act of devotion, the figure is made of wood, I think, but is the colour of iron. It stains the forest's innocence. Harry genuflects before it, but I turn away.

Yes, I say, somebody died. But I add nothing about my mother. I don't want to hear him prattle about eternal rest or see him point up to the pierced god as a symbol of life. I find more comfort in knowing nothing. Uncertainty is my hope against things passing away.

Around us the black trunks turn the forest to a charred cathedral. Harry is still talking, but I am listening to my mother's voice in my head – soothing, humorous – and think that in me, at least, she is alive. Then the bell rings for morning service, so that Harry straightens like a soldier hearing a bugle, and leaves me in a flurry of inconclusion and a trace still of pity.

The sun emerges and lights up a snow of garlic-flowers under the pines. For a while I wander the gullies over decayed log bridges, then return to the friary orchard. A few other guests are about: long-term residents mostly, who look frail – in mourning, or in retreat. We nod and murmur at one another, try no contact.

After a few minutes I reach the end of the lime avenue where a gate leads into the graveyard and the hills rise misted beyond. And it is here, as the cemetery cross lifts into view and the gatepost curves rough under my hand, that I realise my memory is returning. It comes not in blurred fragments, as I had expected, but like a great lake breaking open inside me. Perhaps it has been accessible for long minutes, and I have only just found it. The memories arrive with vivid solidity and fullness. It's as if my internal organs were being restored. Each realisation carries a charge of healing and a tinge of fear. Although recent ones stay buried, I watch almost a year peeling back, and even the pain of it – my mother's weakening voice – carries a tremor of reconciliation, because the emotions too are old and absorbed already, and I recognise them, and they perhaps start to explain me.

8

That year had brought disillusion with my colleagues. It came for no specific reason, but like a vague malaise. Intellectually clever, even outstanding, half the supervising professors were self-important, tired or pedantic. It was the year of the dispute between Agate and Wertheim about the origin of quasars, and their cliques separated off in the canteen like barons for the Wars of the Roses. The two men abraded each other with ritual politeness in the columns of *Nature* and the *Astrophysical Journal*. In the observatory they communicated by memo. They were brilliant and ridiculous. Sometimes I imagined their dispute had nothing to do with quasars at all. They would have disagreed about hemlines or parrot-breeding. Agate – plump, dapper, synthetic – exhaled watchfulness and insecurity. Wertheim I would sometimes see in the car-park – a myopic giraffe of a man – thrusting his key into the wrong Volkswagen.

I developed a defensive antipathy to my supervisor too, who once accosted me with: '*You have an irresponsible imagination.*' Then I realised that he was bemused by me, alarmed. It was familiar from my undergraduate days. I seem to threaten people. I was always called difficult or obstinate or oversensitive. But I think I just hadn't become a cipher. In the observatory half the staff behaved like superior technicians, and I was starting to look back at university with nostalgia, as a time of intellectual excitement. A bad sign. Sometimes, especially at night, I would see from my office window the huge white dish of the telescope, spotlit, turning, and imagine that we'd become its creatures – Wertheim, Agate, all of us – pygmies of vanity and neuroses, spilt out of its bowl like radio signals from nowhere very interesting.

But my own project kept me alive. And how miraculous! In the three seconds after emerging from the lime avenue, as I stand by the cemetery gate, I have garnered ten months' research. All my groundwork now floods back to me, and touches me with astonishment, as if I'd never considered it objectively before. But out in the constellation Lepus, 43,000 light-years away, a red supergiant is circling a void. Already I knew its spectral type and orbital velocity, and was calculating its separation from its dark companion. Scarcely a person on earth, I realised, suspected or cared if it existed. But I was measuring a black hole whose mass was four times greater than the Sun's. How could I have forgotten the wonder of this? Yet I don't know how it ended. Perhaps it was discredited. It isn't lost, of course; but it's not enough that it's stored in my computer at Brabourne, or already published by the International Astronomical Union. I want to recover it in my blood. It's like an obliterated intimacy.

I remember the morning when I began to suspect that the dead star's mass would confirm it as a black hole. I had twinned the diagram of its orbital velocity with that of the supergiant – they dovetailed perfectly – and was scanning the screen for any discrepancy. But the harmony of their approach and recession was beautiful in its way, like music, and nothing deflected it.

I went out for a few minutes and walked in the parkland, at peace with the trees, the sun, because just then everything seemed benign, and rabbits were loping along the garden's edges, and a bronze pheasant gleamed in the grass. As I returned I heard a raucous burst of laughter, and saw the new girl from the Cambridge observatory studying the sundial on the lawn. She was alone, but at this distance still indistinct: just a silhouette, laughing, with blonde lights in her hair.

My hand on the cemetery gatepost attaches me to the world. Its knuckles and veins are all that hold me. The intensity of this remembrance, its beauty and relief, detaches me from my body, which winces enigmatically (what is hurting it?) and covers all track of time. I walked over to her casually (this astonishes me now) and she half turned and I noticed her rather fierce slenderness and the sculptural tension of her face whose features – arched nose, high cheekbones – looked too strong for their voile of skin.

I try to isolate and hold you in my eye – the silhouette, laughing – to see you as I did before my later memory coloured you. I recall a woman businesslike in a denim suit and white blouse. I thought you too scrawny and tense. But I remember your eyes, still glittering with their solitary laughter, and how they seemed, by some sleight of their eyelids and make-up, to tilt up at the corners. But in fact it is impossible to disconnect this moment from all the later ones which swarm in, so that even in this spuriously pristine state you are steeped in my later experience of you, and I have lost even the way you looked round at me: the woman I had not yet kissed.

Sometimes I've doubted that I would ever recover you.

Instead I heard her laughter – harsh and unexpected, like the cry of a peacock out of its beauty. Something had ignited her delight in human absurdity. She jerked her head back at the huge radio dish behind us, and her voice was low and quite disconnected from its laugh. 'The observatory telescope has a resolution of .002 of a second of arc, yet its sundial is *three quarters of an hour* out! Isn't that wonderful?'

So I find her at last. But this relief is airy, unreal. I'm trembling. I can't stop it. My love and apprehension seem inseparable. I don't know how long I've been standing by the cemetery, or who I'm afraid of. The throbbing has started up between my eyes, as if a marksman had drawn a bead there.

But she is secure in me. It's only an amnesiac's fear that his memories will be lost again, that's all. But she will not be lost. Never again. Never. Her name is Jaqueline Everard. She's attached to Professor Hulton's unit at the observatory. She has a flat in the village seven miles away. She goes to bed with her earrings on. Sometimes she talks in her sleep. Her father is dead, she is estranged from her mother. She is challenging, self-willed and arrogant (like me). She was a schoolgirl fencing champion. But she's frightened of centipedes. She has legs like a beautiful deer. She got a 2.1 in natural sciences at Cambridge. She wants to die at fifty. She should have got a First but she had too many theories of her own. We made love under the stars in Sulawesi. She was born on a New Year's Day . . . .

'But perhaps the sundial is right and the sun is wrong. In Cambridge they'd argue that.' She started to walk back across the lawn. 'You're one of the black hole students, aren't you?' She thrust out her hand, suddenly formal. 'I'm with Hulton.'

'And what's that like?'

She went with a long, light stride: impatient energy. 'He's clever, and he doesn't condescend to me for being the wrong sex. That's enough. I don't want pampering.' I believed her. 'And how about you?'

I roughed out my project for her, omitting several misjudgements, so that it became a death-march towards identification and success. She toyed with this a little distrustfully. Her tone was at once thoughtful and faintly mocking. Then she sent down a shower of questions, of which some were playful but one or two disruptively relevant. At last, as we entered the observatory, she let out her earthy laugh and said: 'I think your black hole's just a neutron star!'

I remember how she said this – how her voice hauntingly broke register – and the way she looked at me, very direct and concentrated, yet her lips curled in humour. Later I wondered if I'd seemed impetuous to her, and if she was cautioning me against disappointment. But I wasn't sure: I didn't know her. In fact I thought her older than she was (I confessed later) and she thought me younger, although we shared an age of twenty-eight. But her words, in their silver sheath, carried a tiny needle of disquiet, which she cannot have intended. I already wanted her esteem.

By the time we reached her workroom she was answering my questions about her assignment. Hulton's office was open-plan, and full of young foreigners on grants and fellowships. Announcements came grinding over the intercom. But she didn't seem to notice. The moment she sat at her work-centre and thrust graphs at me and called up computer programs, she became a nervous charge of enthusiasm. I recognised this obsession, because it was mine too: how she loved the unfolding of data into patterns, the countervailing challenge of discovery and surprise, and always in the background the knowledge that our fragile spectra and equations were the voice of things burning thousands of light-years off, whole galaxies observable in the sky only as pinheads of fire. I found myself welcoming this passion of hers, her elated outbursts, as something I'd been missing. Even her ambition seemed to sanction my own.

Her project, I remember, concerned an ancient and massive star – a blue supergiant in Sanduleak – which died a spectacular death in the heart of the large Magellanic Cloud in 1987. Its nuclear fuel exhausted, it collapsed inward on its own core then exploded in gaseous debris which within ten hours had reached a depth of 200 million miles. (She remembered as an undergraduate finding its white glow in the night sky.) By now this obscure star, after its death as the brightest supernova in four centuries, had dwindled to an insignificant neutron star. But within two years, she calculated, the wreck of Sanduleak would shine again. The outrush of its ruins would collide with an older, sleepier ring of gas sloughed during the star's million-year senility and still drifting into space. It was this impact – its surge of radio and X-ray signals and infra-red radiation, its posthumous incandescence of gas and dust – which she anticipated almost with gaiety, like a child awaiting a firework display.

'Look. Look.' She screened up a false-colour satellite image. 'Isn't it beautiful?'

I looked. These pictures from the Hubble's Faint Object Camera can fill you with a dazed sickness, their objects so far away. And now this spent supernova, shining from a galaxy beyond our own, hovered in the dark of her screen as a broken circlet of green and gold. As yet the exploding core was only a yellow billiard-ball suspended in nothing, and the fragments of the circumstellar ring surrounded it untouched. But not for long, she said.

'You remember the Chinese logged the brightest known supernova in 1006? It vanishes from record, then they reported it shining again ten years later! It must be the same phenomenon. Collision with an early ring.' She loved the sheer drama of it. She appeared to be willing the explosion forward. I could not help furtively studying her profile to unravel its eyes' illusion of tilting up. Then she pointed to an engraving pinned to the wall behind her. 'There's my hero.'

That was typical, I suspected. It was a portrait of the seventeenth-century astronomer Simon Marius. It showed the face of a troubled villain, dark, formidable, nested in beard and Vandyke collar. So even Galileo wasn't renegade enough for her, I thought. She had to adopt his arch-foe Marius, 'enemy of all mankind', who claimed to have invented the telescope.

'Galileo called him a reptile, but in fact he was a brilliant observer. He recorded the rebirth of a supernova forty years after its explosion. It faded away within a year. But it was the same process: collision with an earlier gas-ring.'

She had a rooted distrust of reverence, especially in astronomy. Her intellect was too restless and demanding to leave idols intact. But in the next few weeks, every time I encountered her, she unwittingly diversified the woman I had first perceived; I found not one, but many, Jaquelines, who each made the first more complex, like tracings superimposed on one another, until the person I at last took in my arms felt as unpredictable as a water-current.

Apart from my supervisor, Darby, she was the only one who dropped into my office on whim. Her visits stimulated me, just as his depressed. I remember how once his head appeared over my shoulder like an examiner's – his pate reminded me of raw ham – while he scrutinised in silence the data I was studying. He was looking for something to criticise. I think he wanted to make me afraid of him. By now we had developed one of those intangible and apparently causeless aversions which go too deep for cure. He left without a word.

Five minutes later Jaqueline appeared in his place. It was astonishing and rather wonderful, I remember thinking, that the same gap in the air could receive them both. I was still rumbling with anger at him, while she stared at the digits with bemused curiosity. She was dying to communicate mischief. 'I've just read some news from Mount Roche Observatory. Apparently important reappraisals of data are being undertaken due to *bird droppings*.' Her smile glittered down at me. 'The presence of a new galaxy has been cancelled by the bowels of a house sparrow.'

My voice sounded surly to me. 'Did you make that up?'

'No.' Then she caught sight of herself reflected in the window. 'Christ I look a mess.'

'What's wrong?'

'I didn't sleep.'

She appeared genuinely put out. I even sensed her disappointment at failing to cheer me up. For the first time I thought: she likes me.

She said: 'I think the man in the flat above mine is psychopathic. He's got that mania about collecting, so his rooms are piled with stuff he's found in rubbish bins. He never sleeps.'

'Are you frightened?' I couldn't imagine this.

'No, I'm irritated and a bit curious. I'm not kept awake by noises exactly – he hardly makes any – but by what they mean. Tiny scrapings and tinklings. So I wonder: what the hell's he doing up there?'

I thought with surprise: so she sleeps alone. Somehow I'd imagined a boyfriend almost as part of her equipment. His absence made her a little mysterious.

She went on: 'Last night I had the idea he was playing the sitar. I imagined he'd found an orchestra of ruined instruments in a rubbish dump. I lay awake waiting for the next one.' She laughed and dashed her fingers through her hair. 'So today I'm a wreck.'

I said: 'You look fine to me.'

'Do I? I feel vile.' Then she turned her face to mine and smiled, and I had the odd idea that it was an act of intentional self-exposure, as if she were saying: 'This is me at my worst. What do you think?' The stark, open features and slanted eyes were suddenly, dazingly, close to me. I smelt a trace of scent. Then I felt something dislocate inside me – I was reminded of a string snapping. It was as if she entered some more vivid and sensitised dimension: a change as precise as that produced by a first kiss. Nothing had outwardly happened, and she was (she said later) quite unaware of it. But I think that at this moment I started to love her.

She interpreted my silence as depression, and tried to cheer me up again. She had just seen my supervisor in the canteen, and mimicked the way he slurped coffee, spluttering imaginary drops onto the floor. 'Then two Taiwan students came in with a petition to banish the observatory dog. What a hope! I told them you could bring a petition against something insignificant, like a professor, but not against a *dog*. Dogs were inviolate, I said. This was *England*. One of them looked at me quite severely and said: "*This dog not in violet. This dog very disgusting. Has worms. This dog been seen four times dragging its bottom. We are scientists, not vets. This dog . . . .*" '

The ludicrous story continued – I think she invented half of it – while I became distracted by her physical closeness, how warm and light she appeared. I found myself staring at her left hand, which had come to rest on the table's edge beside me. I felt a belated surprise that it carried no ring. Her hands were beautiful: lean and delicately veined. I must have looked too long, because she said: 'Is something wrong?'

'No, nothing.'

She splayed the hand in front of her without comment, and gazed back at the computer screen. She suddenly said: 'I wonder if we're mad.'

I thought, for some reason, that she was alluding to the astronomer's old unease: that we indulged ourselves interpreting the galaxies, while

83

our own planet starved.

But she said: 'No. I've been through that.'

'So we're not mad!' I felt ebullient, but it had nothing to do with the stars. 'We're increasing the world's stock of sanity!'

She seemed not to hear. She just said: 'You know, last night, when I couldn't sleep and went out walking, the stars looked much closer. Of course I've been studying things outside our galaxy, outside optical range altogether. And suddenly these other stars – Sirius, Orion and the rest – seemed prosaic.' She walked to the door. 'Do you think that's terrible?' Then she said almost vaguely: 'You know, the Inuit thought the stars were seal-hunters who had lost their way home.'

I thought she was joking. 'Were they?'

But she only said: 'Possibly.'

And all the time that I've been crossing the light-years between Sanduleak and Lepus and Jaqueline, my hands have been clasping the gatepost by the cemetery – its splinters smart under my fingernails – and I don't know how long I've been standing here, an hour or an instant, with the hills beyond adrift in mist, and the past erupting in me, the monks lying under the earth and Harry still at prayer. I'm pouring sweat. I sit down in the grass replenished, exhausted, folding my arms over my stomach as if I've given birth to her. In a way I have. Places I thought she'd never been are suddenly inhabited by her. She is walking in the Pewsey fields wearing foxgloves on her fingers. Her fierce, laughing intelligence redeems the observatory. Now she is bandaging my ankle for something. Her laughter has grown gentler. She is curled around my thighs in love.

I'm afraid too (otherwise, why this throbbing?).

84

I won't go to her before I remember (remember why I am not living with her, did my illness drive her away?). Between my last memory and now, I think, stretches a desert of fourteen months. I'll cross it soon, whatever I've done, whatever was done to me – or even if nothing happened at all, just the degeneration of feeling, the ebbing away. How could I not know?

She is lying on the black sand of Sulawesi. Her fingers on my shoulders dab a mosquito bite. The trivial memories are infinite. What has happened to you?

9

I am suffering from associative amnesia, the neurologist says. It somehow sounds cowardly. But the usual causes she cites – epilepsy, alcohol, drug addiction – don't apply to me. Even the classical symptoms of depression – loss of sleep or appetite – dog me only intermittently, and generally follow this nervous malaise which seeps up from nowhere.

'You still have a fourteen-month memory loss?' She looks at me without distrust or sympathy: just a neutral face enclosed in severely-parted grey hair, like an ageing ballerina. 'Are there no islands of recall in it?'

'No, I think it's total.' But it's impossible to know. Too many memories float undated.

She writes this down. 'Do you find some of your recovered memories disturbing?'

'No.' Do I? If I do, there's no reason. 'Some are wonderful.'

'But you're suffering stress.'

I still my hands. 'I've lost over a year of my life.'

'You haven't lost it. You've lived it.' Her voice sharpens while her face stays the same. 'It's shaped you. It's inside you.'

I say: 'How do I know that?'

'You need to give yourself time. I don't think you suffer from any major psychiatric illness. Your memory should return within another few days.'

86

But the words jar me. Suddenly, to my surprise, I'm unsure if I want it to return. There's cold air fanning up from my stomach. The reports on her desk make me feel a child. Who has written them? My GP, I suppose, and the foxy houseman. She has spoken to my father, of course, perhaps even to Naomi, to Jaqueline. Everyone knows more of me than I do.

I say: 'You've talked to people who know me.' It's hard to keep the belligerence out of my voice.

'Sometimes it's the best way to reach some understanding. You must realise that.' She rests her forearms over the papers, as if I might read them. 'Why does it make you uneasy?' A stupid question; and I don't answer. 'Have your relationships made you feel anxious?'

I say angrily: 'What relationships?'

'With women.'

'I don't remember enough. I don't even remember how things ended with Jaqueline.' She doesn't query or flinch at the name. Her private knowledge increases my temper. 'I've even forgotten the woman I'm meant to be living with.' I'm starting to shake. I wonder: how culpable is somebody who's forgotten his crime? Could he be sentenced and condemned without memory? What, then, is being punished?

The neurologist says: 'You say you feel guilty?'

I'm still angry, but I answer: 'Frightened.'

'Have the new memories provoked that?'

'I don't know.' The sheaf of reports seems to blanch under her elbows. I think: everything is there. Why doesn't she just tell me?

She says: 'What do you remember of Jaqueline?'

'Happiness.' But the word sounds lonely,

vulnerable. I regret saying it. Suddenly I want to be left in peace. Perhaps I will go away somewhere, anywhere. Yet I hear myself demand: 'You've got a police report there?'

'Oh no.' A trace of sympathy appears in her face. It makes me uneasy. 'Why did you think that?'

'I don't know what I've done.'

She says quite kindly: 'You have no police record.'

The relief I feel seems irrelevant. This inner trembling goes on. Nothing seems to put it to sleep.

She says: 'What's happened has taken place inside you.' She brushes the reports with the back of her hand, as if they were pointless. 'I'm not going to prescribe truth drugs or even Valium – we don't recommend that regularly any more. But I'm ordering tests as a precaution. One of them measures the electric activity in the brain – it chiefly detects epilepsy. The other is a magnetic scanner which exposes vascular trouble. But I don't expect either to uncover anything.' For the first time she smiles, and she looks quaintly virginal, as if her authority were a mask. 'I think you'll recover on your own.'

I stand up to go. I feel tired, after this shadow-boxing. But I remember to ask: 'Is it possible to dream about something the mind has suppressed? Do dreams escape amnesia?'

She says: 'You ask a very difficult thing. I don't know.'

But last night I dreamt that I had discovered a new star in Andromeda. It hung impossibly before my eye and somehow I knew, without a spectroscope, that its bluish brilliance proclaimed an

O-type star which everyone had overlooked. Then over my shoulder a deadened voice, peculiarly painful – it must have been my supervisor's (or perhaps it was Jaqueline's) – said: 'Go back to your figures. It doesn't exist.' And as I looked it contracted to a hard, fluorescent disc and faded away in the night. It was as if the darkness had become viscous and had choked it, and the ache of its going was like the loss of something intimate, something exclusive to me. I even woke up shouting: 'Come back!'

The nurse inscribes crosses on my head with a Chinagraph pencil. Her hands are very small. I feel I'm being measured for a wig or a death-mask, and try to relax by joking. Often all I can hear is her tinkling laughter while behind me she writes her tiny signs or rubs paste into my scalp to loosen its skin resistance. Then she talks in a pattering monotone, perhaps to calm me. 'When was your last meal? . . . That's to check blood sugar . . . . Are you under medication? . . .'

Often I feel my memories sunk inaccessibly deep, but now they seem to tingle beneath my skull, as if her fingers might spark them to life. Then, one by one, she attaches the electrodes to me. They cover my head above the ear-line, dangling from blobs of white paste. There are twenty-two of them, so that I joke about two football teams playing across my scalp; but my voice sounds tense and her laughter tightens. She guides me to a deeper chair, carrying behind me the box where the electrode wires terminate, so that for a moment we process together in foolish majesty, as if preserving a precious crown or hairstyle.

I sit on the chair's edge. She says: 'Relax. Open your mouth. Gently. Relax . . . .' She is standing behind a processing unit now, and soon I hear the faint, jittery tapping of its twenty-two pens, recording I don't know what: a noise like mice feeding. I watch her while she scans the graph. From time to time she says: 'Close your eyes . . . open your eyes . . . .' and whenever I open them I imagine that the expression on her face has become newly troubled. But in fact it is only businesslike, I think, and a little bored. 'Close your eyes again . . . .'

I daren't move my head because the electrodes drape it like spaghetti. The whole process seems primitive. Yet I imagine my memories leaking out unknown to me along the wires, and that the near-soundless pens are recording them for the nurse, so that when she says 'Open your eyes again' I fancy a fleeting horror on her face, and wonder what she's just read.

But later, after it is over, I see these elaborate electroencephalograms. They mean nothing to me. I only try to decode her face as she starts to fold them up: twenty-two ranges of ugly peaks and dips, like cross-sections of landscape. But her expression stays cloudless and young. So I stab my finger at a place where a sudden chasm plunges off the graph. She says: 'That's when you blinked . . . .'

I point at others. 'What about that? . . . and that?'

'That is where you closed your eyes . . . . This is where you opened them. The fuzzy areas show anxiety, muscular interference.'

'And what's that?' I point to the lowest line: a procession of spikes like a fakir's bed.

'That's your heartbeat.'

The delicacy of my internal machinery is newly alarming. But I ask: 'What about my brain?'

She says: 'The frequency should be the same in both hemispheres.' Her tinkling laughter re-appears. 'So we hope your football teams draw!'

'Do they?'

'I'm afraid I can't tell you. It's up to the consultant to interpret them.'

'But you're the technician. I think you know.'

'I can't be sure at all. You mustn't quote me.' She pauses and looks at me. I don't know what she sees. I feel detached. Her lips look too callow for my fate to hang on. She only says: 'I don't think you need worry.' Then she peers through the door's glass panel. 'The radiographer has come for your brain scan.'

I follow him down to the basement, where the machine sits ostracised in its own room. It is a huge magnet, he says, which will take deep resonance images of the brain. But it resembles an outsize washing-machine, where people are spun dry. Before entering its tunnel I am divested of my watch, credit card, coins, even a stray paper-clip. The nurses are tender with me. In their control unit I glimpse photographic negatives of internal organs hung up in cross-section like sliced meat.

I'm ushered through a heavy door. The room is a self-contained magnetic field, where a moving platform carries the patient into the tunnel, as a corpse is borne away inside a crematorium. I know that it is designed to detect tumours and blood clots, but I cannot stop the idea that instead it lays bare memories, and suddenly I'm afraid of it. A nurse takes my hand while I lie on the platform. Somewhere from behind, the coil is eased over my head like a metal cage. The nurse says something soothing. For a second my palm is sweating in hers. As the platform lifts and carries me into the hole, I am struck by momentary panic. I have the fear that I will be reduced to pure memories. Nothing holds me to the world but the little periscope mirror above my head, placed so that a patient can see his relatives seated on a sofa at the end of the room. But the sofa is empty. I want to cry out, but don't. I stay in silence, staring through the mirror down the ellipse of light where my legs obtrude like someone else's. A voice comes dulled through my ear-plugs: 'Stay calm, Mr Sanders. We'll be starting the program in a few seconds.'

I wait. Beyond the sofa I see the window of the control room, where the radiographer's head is examining a screen. But it is only a silhouette. For a few seconds I hear my own heart. Then the noise starts in muffled reverberations all over the tunnel wall above me. It is as if workmen were drilling a road close above: not loud, but diffused and penetrating, even through the ear-plugs, until it dins inside my head. I know it does not peel back memory. I know. Yet I feel it thinning away my skull. There's almost nothing between it and whatever festers beneath. It goes on and on. I want to say something to the control room, but I feel a fool. What can I claim? That my memory is coming back, and I'm frightened? That I don't want to be cured?

The voice over the speaker says: 'Is everything all right, Mr Sanders?'

'Yes.'

No, it is not all right. Somebody else should be under this scanner: somebody who wants their tumour out, their memory back. But my body is shaking (can't they see?). I want to stay with the memories I have. Just for another day, an hour. With her. As she is, as I was. I must be a coward after all. I close my eyes against the noise, the sofa, all thinking.

Sometimes the dinning stops while they change the program. Then once more I hear the thump of my heart, and I expect my memories to burst like ulcers into my conscious. But instead the noise starts up again, abrading my skull, inflaming the past. And all the time I know it's an illusion, and that the machine is harmlessly recording; yet I go on willing the carapace of bone to stand firm, to hold back time, to preserve whatever is myself.

10

At the celestial equator, where the stars of the southern hemisphere crowd to meet those of the north, the skies glitter with greater complexity. Familiar reference points wheel away. Nothing new shines with the precision of the Great Bear or Orion. Instead the constellations appear to burn with a cold, even brilliance. Farther south you can gaze down the funnel of the whole Milky Way, and glimpse the white dust of the Magellanic Clouds.

I would never have dreamed of coming here. I had never travelled beyond Italy before. It was she, of course, who compelled me, with her love of the remote and outlandish, and her disdain for obstacles. 'Let's try Indonesia!' She seemed to inhabit so easily wherever she was.

In the sultry nights, when we slept on the hotel roof, the stars glimmered with a stifled, reddish light, as if the swelter choked them. Sometimes the flares of a fishing-boat glided detached over the Sulawesi Sea. Standing up, she asked: 'What do you imagine they thought – primitive men – when they looked up and saw all those lights?' She walked to the edge of the roof, quite naked. 'Probably they imagined fireflies.' She cupped her hands around her eyes, to exclude the glare of the lamps in the garden below. And there she remained for a while, leaving herself on my memory, standing like a primitive worshipper on the roof-edge. 'When I was a girl I wanted the stars for *myself*. Isn't that typical? They weren't in the least mysterious.'

I thought of the hushed nights in my father's observatory, the planets turning in the dark. Their strangeness had never quite deserted me, even at university. I said: 'How on earth did you take to astronomy then?'

'I thought of it as an extension of physics. It was just something I was good at. Most people are like that, aren't they? We do what we're already good at. We're technicians. Does that sound immoral?' She came over, stooped and kissed me. 'I might have been good at manufacturing arms, then I'd have done that!'

I did not always know whether she was mocking herself or me. Her outspokenness was sometimes painful. Even her body, standing above me in the dark, reflected this high-spirited abandon: a beautiful, purpose-built body which moved with its own economy.

I pulled her down against me. 'You're joking.'

'Not at all. My mother used to say I didn't give a damn if a thing was good or bad, just if it was true. I was the family lie-detector. But you—' She withdrew her face a little to stare at mine. 'You're different. Maybe you secretly believe in God.' She laughed her guttural laugh. 'The mystery to me isn't stars, but people. How some of them are happy. How they stick with boring husbands and wives and put up with mutinous children. I can guess at the origin of quasars, but I don't understand happiness.'

I wondered if she was covertly telling me something, staking out her independence; because already I was beginning to see that I could marry her. I said simply: 'But we're happy.'

'Happiness.' Her hands caressed my shoulders. 'Doesn't it sound like a reversion to infancy? It's the end of experience.' She was smiling, kissing me. ' "The pursuit of happiness", as if it was a fox!' But the tilted eyes were glittering over me, and her kisses spattered my neck and chest. 'It's a chimera. It's just a side-effect.'

'So it does exist.'

She didn't answer. Our bodies stuck together in the humid dark. But she extracted an arm from under mine and extended it at the sky. 'Things up there are comparatively simple!'

She may have held this gesture for only a second, but in the random way of memory I have turned her to statued marble. Her profiled face, her arm and lifted breast included a kind of pathos which I did not understand. Sometimes I think I do not know her at all.

The gesture returns (unless my mind repeated it) as our outrigger moves over a waveless sea. 'Look! Dolphins!' Her arm flung out to starboard followed the glisten of bodies just breaking the surface. 'How beautiful!' And there they were – the legendary man-lovers – curveting between air and water. After a minute they swam alongside like torpedoes, but supple and vulnerable, with barred sunlight stippling their backs. Then they were gone.

'That's good luck!' She looked happy.

The divemaster seated opposite us said: 'Spirits.'

To either side the sea simmered in a tranquil plain. The shafts of the outrigger – saplings lashed together – skimmed and sliced it in cruel rhythm. I felt as though I'd strayed into a travel brochure. In front of us, an island-volcano lifted from the sea, plumed with perpendicular cloud as if it had just erupted.

'That one's finished,' the divemaster said. 'Nothing left.' He was burly, but his face looked blank and dazzled as if he'd spent all his life smiling at the sea. His legs were discoloured by coral scars. 'Those the dangerous ones: Lokon, Mahawu.' He pointed astern. 'They change all the time.' He was looking across the water beyond jungled hills, to where twin volcanoes were boiling in grey-white cumulus.

Jaqueline smiled. 'We'll climb one.'

'It's forbidden,' the man said. 'The government forbid it. Last year a Swiss lady scientist died there, in Lokon.'

'How?'

'Nobody knows. Her body never found.'

'Then we'll climb Mahawu.'

'Mahawu worse. Its water almost gone. Mahawu will erupt any day soon. Last year two men die there, but government didn't forbid.' He grinned. 'They were only local people.'

The outrigger stammered to a halt, and we cast anchor. Beneath us, through the turquoise water, we could see the curve of the coral wall echoing the coast and almost as clear. We looked down a hundred feet as if at our hands. Only when the divemaster heaved out the air cylinders and inflatable jackets, I felt a twinge of unease. I had dived just once before, but Jaqueline was amphibious: as a girl she had dived in Tenerife and the Red Sea. She laughed at me when I mistook my depth gauge for the compressed air dial. But as we perched on the boat's side, she checked my regulator and asked the man to change my mask. 'I don't like the look of it. This equipment's awful.'

Over the tingle of my nerves her solicitude sent a warm calm. I loved her confidence. She was beyond my protection, or anyone's. And as we submerged, the divemaster leading, I could sense her eyes on me, darkened behind their mask. Because I was breathing fast and light, I did not descend as I should, and her hand arrived on mine and began gently to pull me down, down the harlequin lustre of the coral wall, the swarming shoals, down where the water had polished everything to a still, fragile clarity.

I had seen nothing like it. The whole reef palisade, as we began to swim, became a coruscating mass of brilliant and intricate shapes. Among the silver ferns and sponges drifted thousands of tiny fish – magenta, peach, black. At first we pointed them out for one another, then we gave up. The whole wall was fissured with petrified flowers, sea-fans, gorgonians and starfish, and perforated by the soundless trumpets of cup-coral. If we looked up we saw whole shoals suspended and translucent against the sunlight, while beneath us, clear of the vertiginous wall, throngs of angelfish and lyretails were spun out in thin air.

Once we gathered at the lair of a mantis shrimp – a tangle of multi-coloured claws and feelers – and our masks clashed as we pulled out our regulators and kissed. Then we were swimming again, in the intimacy of our slight, shared danger, and the sensation of flying returned.

I imagined that everyone was looking at her. Only

the fish sweeping blindly against us could be indifferent! In the village markets, from their aisles of unfamiliar spices, the dark women would hail us smiling and touch their fingers to their eyes or hair. In my eyes, too, she fell into some rarer focus, because her questing energy isolated her here. Even as she joked in sign language, she was pervaded by some restless, commanding quality, which made the men, in particular, look at her bemused.

Once a schoolmaster, sporting a red parasol, invited us to his home. He was proud of his English, I think, proud of his hospitality, intrigued by our strangeness. Jaqueline, in particular, fascinated him. He could not take his eyes off her. 'In your country,' he asked, 'do all the women look like Madam?'

'No,' I said proudly, 'no.'

Seated under the slatted roof of his balcony, we escaped the noon blaze while his family crowded round us: a young wife and five barefoot children neat in tomato-coloured school frocks or shorts, a white-haired mother with a mouthful of jumbled teeth. Inside I glimpsed walls of woven rattan and a few bamboo beds and chairs. But children and adults all smiled at us with the same smile – glittering, easy – and offered us coconut juice. They had English-sounding names: Flora, Henry, Nancy. Cradling her new baby, the young wife lowered him towards Jaqueline's lap. Everyone went on smiling while Jaqueline caressed the child as if puzzled by something, and nuzzled his fingertips. I sensed that she, who came from a broken home, was mystified by this sunny, impoverished clan: above all by the young woman whose cheery serenity had effortlessly multiplied in her children.

The schoolmaster brought out sweet biscuits and cold water in a Bintang beer bottle. He said: 'And how do you and your wife like Sulawesi?' It was impossible to tell his age. Scraps of moustache and beard flecked his face as if by accident.

'It's very beautiful,' I said.

'Yes, Sulawesi is very nice.' His voice took on a sing-song rectitude. 'It would be very good for tourists, but few come. It is very interesting and peaceful. Everybody is very happy in Indonesia.'

He had a position in the village, of course, and perhaps it was automatic to honour his country, to misinform. I sensed Jaqueline tighten beside me. We had read the same books, including a pamphlet on national etiquette ('*It is considered bad manners to broach matters of controversy*').

The schoolmaster lifted a glass of wine to us. 'I drink to our countries.' From time to time half his face lurched into a tic, which made him seem involuntarily to wink. 'Tell your friends when you return how picturesque is everything here. They are always welcome in Sulawesi. Here in the north we are Christian, you know. But it is good all over our country. We are a happy people.'

Jaqueline said suddenly: 'How can you be?'

He frowned. 'Madam?'

Momentarily I wanted to preserve her image in him – this pale-eyed beauty so different from his own women: his gaze had been indulging her like an ornament. But she repeated: 'How can you be, after 1965? A million people murdered, perhaps, and nobody speaks of it!'

'A million . . . the figure isn't mine . . . .' He stared back at her, stupefied. His tic intensified. 'You mean the purges? This was . . . . Why should

100

people speak of this?'

'It happened.'

Around us the women continued to smile, uncomprehending, and the small girls in their Alice bands went on smiling too, and the old woman nodded and beamed. None of them understood English. But the schoolmaster got to his feet and said 'We should walk', and we descended the verandah into a little grove of banana palms, the children playing behind us. The man's smile had become a formal rictus, and the pedantry was gone from his voice. He still addressed himself to me, as if I might be a ventriloquist and this woman my dummy. It seemed the only explanation of her. He said: 'It's true those were terrible times.'

Hesitantly I asked: 'What happened here?'

'We don't talk about such things among ourselves now. Nobody does. But I know in the West it is different and you talk.' He stared ahead as we walked, like a soldier on drill. He might have been addressing the palms. 'You're talking about the communist purges, aren't you?'

'Is that what you call them?'

'I was only a boy.' He left another silence: the decision to talk was as conscious as turning a lock. 'These men came to our village. Government men from Java, soldiers and others. I remember we were ordered to gather in the open space by the graveyard. Then they read out a list of communists, atheists and so on. I don't know how they knew these men. Many of them were Chinese, who nobody liked. But others just weren't on the church register, or the imam wouldn't claim them. My father was one.'

Even on the word 'father' his voice stayed

toneless. 'Because we were new in the village, nobody spoke for us. My mother was there too. I remember her hand on my head. The suspects were marched forward and tied together. Then the soldiers ordered the villagers to get clubs and pangahs and kill them in the graveyard. They wanted the people to have blood on them. My mother had a cigarette and told me to put it between my father's lips. I was only six but I remember how his mouth trembled. Then the women and children were ordered back to our houses, and I never saw him again.'

His children were running round us, playing with palm leaves. Jaqueline said: 'So you had to kill your own people?'

The man went on: 'Two of the villagers could not, and the soldiers clubbed them to death. But the others managed it. They had nightmares afterwards, and some committed suicide. This happened all over these islands. For years the ghosts were moving about at night. You could feel them everywhere.' His voice turned breathy. 'We know the man who killed my father. Whenever we passed him in the fields his eyes would turn odd. Later we moved to another village and tried to be new.' He suddenly laughed. 'Such things do not happen in the West.'

'But the West condoned it here,' I said.

Jaqueline exclaimed: 'I'm sorry.'

Ten minutes later, as the family swarmed round us in beaming farewell, she took off her necklace and gave it to the old widow. Returning in a local bus, we were silent. The genial farmers filled the seats around us with their silent history. They chattered and slept. I felt tired and depressed for the first time. But Jaqueline gazed out of the

102

window with replenished interest. I sensed her satisfied, as if some kind of justice had been done. She said: 'Perhaps that is why they have to smile.'

Down the coral rampart the shoals bloomed into thousands. They brushed obliviously against us, as if aeons of evolution had conditioned them to see only themselves. So we ceased to exist. Fantastically spotted and barred, they touched us with cold fins. We were the ghosts of their world.

We were cut off from one another too. Our conversation was reduced to four or five hand-signals, and the rasp of breathing in our regulators was all we could hear, enclosing us in our bodies. It sounded harsh and artificial.

But a subtle companionship attached us. The divemaster swam in front, occasionally pointing out a starfish or a giant clam on the sea-bed. Eventually he seemed to forget us, and we kept watch on one another. The coral wall became private to us. We were reduced to floating eyes. And around us the fish grew ever more phantasmagoric. Sometimes their sleepy multitudes plumed out along the current in processions of phosphorescent blue and silver, sometimes they massed beneath us in shadowy regiments. Just as we thought their variety was exhausted, a new shape or colour would glitter into view. There were fish quartered by clownish purple and tomato bands, or striped horizontally in saffron and rose; slab-like fish with pouting lips which smiled and bumped against us, and others so barnacled they were barely distinguishable from coral; Moorish Idols whose dorsal fins dripped effetely behind them; fish with scowls and leers and meaningless expressions of disgust or surprise; curtains of eel-like creatures hanging vertically all together; parrotfish, damselfish, barracudas. Some hovered almost transparent, as though etched onto crystal. Others flickered around their dens in the half-dead algae and coral, or volleyed out of the sea-ferns in miniature showers. And all the time the blonde-streaked fish with athletic legs, the fish I am in love with, swims in and out of my vision. She would not leave anywhere unexplored, but twisted into miniature canyons and caves so that the divemaster, who was used to being followed, kept impatiently returning.

But sixty feet down the schools of lesser fish thinned away. We started to go deeper. The sun still lit the sea like a vast jewel, but the coral drained of colour and turned dead.

Lying on the black sand in the muffled night, I remember wondering why she never said 'I love you'.

Love. The word can mean anything (she said). I know I want you, I like you – isn't that enough? But 'love' stakes claims out of need.

The words are hers, not mine (mine were different, helpless). She said: 'Love is need, isn't it? In the end. And what's wrong with that?'

'You enjoy confusing me.'

'I? I'm the least confusing person in the world!' She cradled my head, sucked my mouth. 'Is this confusing you?'

'Yes . . . .'

She said: 'You're looking for the wrong certainties, Edward. The world isn't like that, haven't you noticed?'

104

She sprinkled the sand laughing on my chest. 'Does black sand confuse you?' Then her head came smiling above me, dark against the stars and the mangrove trees, her eyes shining in it. They gleam new-washed in my memory. I leant up and kissed them, because I wanted them shut. They seemed at the core of my confusion. Sometimes, dazed by them, I wondered: were they just a physical accident? But no, they were perhaps her heart: grey-blue organs of intelligence and control. How could she wear them so nakedly?

I heard myself say: 'Whose eyes are those?'

'My father's. Most things about me are my father's.'

She had scarcely spoken of him. He had been less a person than an absence: a lawyer who abandoned her mother when his daughter was nine, and emigrated to Canada. 'You didn't love him.'

'I didn't know him. He was selfish, arrogant and clever.' She spoke the words evenly, as of equal qualities. 'I hardly saw him after he left. I don't blame him. My mother was impossible, still is.'

Her childhood was cruelly romantic to me. Where mine had been spent in a sensitised dream, bathed in my parents' affection under the Pewsey hills, hers showed a rack of conflict and isolation: a social London home in which her brothers excluded her and her mother was turning to drink. She had never taken me to visit this mother, and rarely did herself. She described a wealthy, formidable yet superficial woman, who regarded her children as part of her catastrophe at the hands of an unforgivable man. A professional victim, she was yet domineering and vain. Jaqueline spoke of her with hot contempt.

'All my childhood I remember her distracted by

impractical schemes. First she tried interior decoration, then she wanted to become a painter, then get her voice trained – it was too late – then practise landscape gardening. The one thing she stuck to was astrology. It started as a pastime, then it became a mania. I remember this silliness all through my schooldays. She wielded its authority like a religion. We couldn't question it, just as we couldn't mention my father. But whenever I showed signs of rebellion she'd say 'That's your father in you' – and it was like a curse. As a girl I thought I must be tainted. I couldn't escape his blood. Later it made me fantasise and long for him. But he wasn't there, of course. He was just a stillborn part of me.'

She had lain down beside me on the sand again, and was talking to the sky. The sea rippled metallically near our feet. I said: 'Did he never contact you?'

'Later he swore he'd written letters to us. My mother may have torn them up, or he may have been lying, I don't know. She got worse and worse. Whenever she wanted to convince or frustrate us, she'd cast a horary chart, declaiming about Saturn transiting Mars or the progressed Sun being conjunct with Mercury. This would mean we could or couldn't go to parties, receive birthday presents or buy a dog. Even when we passed exams it was because of planetary conjunctions. If my stubbornness wasn't due to my father's blood in me it was because at my birth the Libran Sun manifested itself through Ascendant Scorpio, or some rot.' Anger had obliterated her humour, and thickened her voice.

'Is that why you took to astronomy – to clean away all that?'

'Partly, yes. I wanted to overcome her.' Her face turned to me over the sand. Her mouth drifted through my hair. 'It was like achieving sanity. Perhaps a kind of revenge.'

'But you're the sanest person I know!' I wondered what this refutation of her mother had cost her. My own was too different: her love unconditional, just the outcome of her nature. Jaqueline's mother was unimaginable to me.

She said: 'I'm only sane through will-power. When I was seventeen I changed myself. It was a conscious decision. I decided that everything my mother was, I wouldn't be. So I recreated myself. I even threw away half my clothes, and changed to my middle name. I used to be Rosamund – didn't I tell you that?'

I propped myself on my elbow and stared at her. I imagined her eleven years before – the quick-witted girl with her proud face and adolescent figure – refusing to be trampled, plotting her future. I stretched out and touched her cheek, the glittering eyes. She awed me a little. I could not meet her gaze without feeling shaken. I just said: 'You're extraordinary.'

'I'm just unlucky.' She was bantering again. 'But I've had the right childhood for a vile world.' She pushed me playfully back and writhed on top of me. 'Unlike you. You're too delicate, Edward, too sensitive. Things upset you.' She was tugging down my trousers.

'Like what?'

'Like me. Sometimes you should just ignore me. My moods.'

'I can't ignore you.'

Her mouth was over mine, and her sinuous body. Her kisses circled my neck. My sex stiffened

107

in her fingers. It is these moments which my memory tries fully to retrieve, and cannot. They blur and elide. The moment of entering her brings this spasm of ecstasy, but then I feel myself burning and diffusing in her, I grow lost, I no longer know where I end and she begins. So I hold her away a little above me, establishing her separateness in the dark: her shoulders, her arms, her hair. I push at her breasts with my palms, feeling her flesh's reality. I tell myself: I am inside this other. It is around me. We cannot be closer. Ever.

I need to hold her away like this in order to know it. Then the rhythmic movements become a warm, muffled labour, indistinct, my memory fails them. I gaze at her until her gentle friction round me makes me come. Then her fingers are over my body again, clasping and kneading in some fever of their own. Her gasping becomes a refrain. Her eyes are closed. I feel as if I've disappeared to her – her loving is often like this – and that she is hunting for something of her own in the dark, or engaged in civil war, until after a while, with a little cry, she sighs into quiet.

Two minutes go by, then she slips off me and walks toward the sea. She halts in the shallows, and her hands come up and sift her hair. And there my memory freezes her again: her dimpled shoulders and the white line left by the bikini across her tanned back, a frisson of leftover desire.

So when I think of her, my most vivid, my most erotic memories frame her apart from me, and it is only by these instants, almost haphazard, that I convince myself she was ever close to me.

So the way her head turned underwater, with lingering solicitude, checking that I was still near her, keeps returning to me with a disquiet which I cannot explain, even as we dropped down the sheer reef wall into the cooler currents, the paled coral. I checked my depth gauge to find us eighty feet down. Above us the shoals made distant constellations against the dimming sun. The coral turned to an ashen jungle, and the gnarled or feathery shapes of polyps and anemone were bleached to ghosts of those coruscating fifty feet above. Their skeletons brushed against our hands. And these depths were patrolled by lone groupers – giant primitives whose lustreless bodies merged with the coral.

Even Jaqueline became faintly unnerved. Instinctively we swam alongside and checked each other's air gauges. Once, at the mouth of a crevasse, a turtle sculled away between us, leisurely and alone out of prehistory. And once, swimming together above a ledge, we looked down and saw a reef-shark twenty feet below. We stopped waveringly, clasped each other's hand. It twisted shyly away. Jaqueline smiled. But we remained there for a moment, suspended upright, holding hands like children.

11

It's been two days since I was here, but it feels like
a year. The house is unchanged, of course, (why
should it change?) and has gathered no memories.
Only the blown hawthorn petals lie newly white
across the orchard, and some guttering has fallen
from the outhouse. Naomi is not here. She has left
a note to say she'll be back soon. It is a relief to be
alone. Some inner pendulum keeps swinging me
between anxiety and indifference, and it is in this
jaded calm that I wander the overgrown drive, the
orchard and the limbo of these unremembered
rooms. I inhabit them more easily now – they are,
for the moment, the only place I can call home –
and the presence of my possessions in them (my
papers strewn over the study, my clothes hanging
beside hers) seems less extraordinary than it did. I
even imagine myself a lodger here.

A year's recovered memory quickens into life.
Possessions previously alien to me – objects which
had left me with a sordid feeling of owning them
second-hand – I now recognise as mine,
purchased in Bristol or London. I suddenly realise
I've read books which were blank to me two days
ago. Rifling through the wardrobe, I see too that a
crimson jacket which I'd assumed to be Naomi's is
one I chose myself, with Jaqueline. ('You dress
like a monk! Buy something that'll clash!') Even
in the kitchen various articles – pewter mugs and

dishes – rejoin me. And a stuffed owl which I'd considered absurd turns out not to be hers, but mine.

I sit in the orangery, waiting for nothing I'm sure of. The geraniums exhale their airless scent. I close my eyes in the weak sunlight. The urge to remember, and the fear of it, have subsided for now. The sensation of battling against fog has gone. Instead I feel as if the past were tingling just beneath my skin, that in a moment – if I neither force nor evade it – it will push up through the last membrane and spread about it a qualified peace.

Seagulls are crying inland. It's a discomfiting sound. Now that I've recovered Jaqueline, I can imagine even less how I came into the home of this other one. I find myself staring at the telephone, wondering if Jaqueline still works at the observatory, and whether to ring her. But now I'm afraid of her voice. I hate my helplessness. In a day or two, when I've recovered, I'll understand our separation: it can only be a crazed mistake. Then I'll return to her.

I do not hear Naomi's car on the drive, only her footsteps hesitating in the passage. She is cloudy to me. I can scarcely remember what she looks like. The kitchen door opens and she carries in her shopping and says 'Hi!'. She is trying to be casual, but her jaw looks tight and her eyes sear me. 'How did things go?' She starts unpacking the food. She keeps her back to me. 'I was worried when you left.'

'You needn't have been. That friary was as quiet as the grave.' But I remember what a fool I'd been with the solicitor's secretary in Dorchester. 'Afterwards I went to the hospital where my father had arranged an appointment. I saw a woman doctor

111

there. Had she spoken with you?'

'Yes, she had.' She looks uneasy.

'What the hell did she want?'

'She wanted to know what your health had been like.'

'You mean my mental health?'

'Yes.'

I try to imagine these two strangers bandying my inner life between them. She is studying me with her disquieting attention. 'What did you tell her?'

'I told her what I've told you. That you've suffered stress and had a kind of breakdown.'

'What else?'

Momentarily she forgets herself and starts: 'Darling . . . ' then throttles the last syllable and turns her head away. 'She wanted to know your background – had you shown symptoms of epilepsy, and so on. I told her no, but that you were sensitive, and nervous sometimes.'

It's like getting a report from a headmistress. 'Nervous? I'm bloody well not.'

'You bloody well are.' But she laughs softly, and it seems to cauterise the thing. 'And what about . . . ?' She drops a packet of biscuits and I notice her hands are trembling. 'What about your memory?'

'It's partially returned.' Again I feel the euphoria of it, a great warmth spreading along my arteries. 'It came quite suddenly. For no reason. It was extraordinary, like a series of rooms opening up inside.'

I am still sitting in the orangery chair, and she is standing in front of me. For some reason I sense that we have often been like this. She is smiling, but taut, as if on mental tiptoe. 'What did you remember?'

'Incidents at the observatory. Holidays.' But I do not want to tell her about Jaqueline. Those times are private to me. They also seem fragile, like things kept isolated in darkness, things which daylight might destroy.

She asks: 'What else did you remember?'

I don't want to hurt her, but I say: 'Not you.'

'No.' Her voice is level, but her eyes so intense. I cannot warm to her. She says: 'You mustn't worry about me. Amnesia's not an insult.' But she looks stricken.

'I recovered almost a year of time,' I tell her. 'I remember up to fourteen months ago.'

She says quietly: 'That's wonderful.'

'It's odd. I see my work in the observatory developing in leaps, like a movie speeded up. But I also see my mother growing iller. That lemon tinge to the skin. She got desperately thin, didn't she?'

'I never knew her.'

'No, of course not.'

She returns to unpacking the shopping. How deeply she entered my life is opaque to me. I glance at her and try to divine what it is I may have loved, and cannot. Simply she is not Jaqueline. She is a walking absence: the space where another should be.

After a moment she says that she's going to try to paint. 'You'll be all right?' She makes her irritating gesture of brushing back absent hair with one hand. But I feel purposeless; I follow her unthinking to the studio. Above its skylight birds are singing. The portrait of the middle-aged woman is still on her easel. I had thought it complete, but I see that she has now textured the hands into a tactile softness. She stares at this, tapping her wrist with a maulstick, frowning.

Behind her back I ease old canvases from their racks. There are portraits half-finished, abandoned, redeveloped. I find the full-length study of an old man – skin of papery fragility, a web of bones. These finished works seem to be discarded among sketches and rejects. I wonder vaguely what shows she has had. She goes on staring at her portrait, displeased by something.

Idly I pull out another canvas, then stop in disbelief. It is a portrait of Jaqueline. Out of its shining pigments, laid on in cruel streaks, she stares back and into herself. Naomi has painted her in chiaroscuro, as if she were sitting across a flood of light. So half the face is clear, its bones high, the eye pale and cool. But the other half is retracted in shadow, so that the whole canvas lurches into sickening schizophrenia. This eye is only a socket, and seems displaced a little downward in the cheek, the features straying into cubism. The mouth makes a scarlet crease. It is a flayed face, but mask-like, settled into some personal torment. It's a portrait blatantly the spawn of jealousy.

I must have let out some noise, because Naomi has turned round.

I hear a voice high with anger, my own. 'What have you done?' I pitch the canvas near her feet. 'When the hell did you do that?'

She looks startled. She just stands there and says: 'That was done ages ago. A year ago.'

'I never even knew you knew her! How long have you known her?'

She has the grace to turn pale. 'I only saw her two or three times. When I first met you. The portrait's done from memory. She never sat for me.'

'That's obvious. You've left out everything! Her beauty, her intelligence, her vitality! That portrait's dead!'

I touch a nerve, and I'm glad: the affronted artist. 'I have a right to my vision.'

'Your vision's a bloody lie!' It's fantastic that she's been concealing all this. So she knows perfectly well who Jaqueline is, what she means to me. And all the time she harbours this voodoo doll of a portrait. I even wonder if she is trying to keep Jaqueline away. This much is flagrant in the portrait: she'd like to annul her. If you wanted to kill somebody's heart, this is the portrait you'd paint. She stands there so pale, so taut, like a sensitised witch, with those black eyes, and I think: Christ, yes, jealousy makes you do anything. And next she has the effrontery to say:

'So you remember her now.' She's gone very quiet.

'Did you hope to keep her dark?'

'Of course not.'

'You obviously hate her. Why didn't you use bile instead of oils? It's a work of pure vengeance. It's nothing like her.'

A flush has entered her cheeks. I think it's anger. Good. She says: 'You recognised it.'

'If you're trying to keep us apart, let me tell you: in a day or two I'm going to pick up the phone and join her.' The words seem to make it possible. 'And why all this secrecy? How long has it been hidden here? How . . . .'

'Oh Edward' – the Christian name unnerving on her lips – 'it wasn't hidden. You've seen it before.' She picks it up and turns it to the wall. 'Before, you didn't like it, but you didn't think it a lie.'

She's looking at me with a kind of appalled compassion. It maddens me. But I can't dispute her. I can't be sure of anything any more. I'm breathing harshly, as if I've sprinted a mile.

She goes on: 'I didn't hate her. I never really knew her. I just painted from instinct. I'm sorry. It was more like an exercise than anything. I sometimes do that. I never thought it would hurt you. I should have destroyed it.'

'It doesn't hurt me.' But it does, it does. 'It hurts her.'

'I'm sorry.' Her fingers are pulling at one another. But what she's sorry for, I'm not sure. I don't understand her.

Then I feel a slow, heavy exhaustion. As suddenly as my anger flared, it's gone; and it leaves behind this bewilderment. Why does it matter so much: a picture by a woman I do not love? I hear myself say: 'Look. In a few days I'll leave here. It'll be better for both of us.'

But she answers: 'Where would you go? You're still unwell. When you recover . . . if you still want to go . . . that's different . . . .'

She smiles faintly. Her eyes travel over me, wondering, and I see myself in them, and feel ashamed. 'I'm sorry, Naomi. I don't know what's happening to me. I didn't mean that about vengeance, about your having tried to keep us apart.'

She says: 'You know I wouldn't do that.'

She's forgotten that I don't know: I don't know anything about her. I say: 'I must be unrecognisable to you.'

'No.' But she still watches me with that look of expectancy, as if at any moment I will turn

116

remembering eyes on her. Instead I feel hot and listless, almost uncaring. After a while her hand arrives on my forearm. 'What are you going to do now? It must be hell. Waiting.'

But I have no idea what to do. The pressure is building up in my head again, but it's familiar now, an old adversary. For the moment I just want to get out of here. I say: 'I think I'll go to my father.'

A shadow of disappointment crosses her. She makes for the kitchen to assemble a picnic lunch, but returns and picks up the canvas. 'I'll throw it away if you want. I didn't much like it.'

'Yes. Throw it away.'

12

I suspect that the memories came alive in me unacknowledged several hours ago, and that the journey to my father impelled them into my thoughts. This is strange: that the recollection of my mother's death has nested in me unnoticed all morning (I think), while I raged at Naomi. But now it comes to me softly, almost without surprise, as I motor through the rain. My body, my emotions, feel no shock: over fourteen months they have accommodated to it. She faded away in her sleep during the night at home. I see my father's face in the morning, unable to say the words, so that I fear he's had a stroke.

I stop in a lay-by while this breaks in on me. From the familiarity of these memories – they must have repeated in my head many times – I realise that I have become used and half reconciled to her absence, and I feel distantly ashamed. That is the sadness of healing grief, that it takes us away from the dead.

Her end had been signalled for days, but nothing prepares you. Our mourning was deadened by shock. There was no wildness of grief, just this muffled inaccessibility to any acute sensation at all. It was bewildering. I imagined that in a day or two her going would be borne in on me and I would give myself over to unrestrained weeping. But nothing happened. Just this numbness, this drunken dissociation, while I sat over my work-station in the observatory and tried to collate figures.

Only occasionally something bypassed my paralysis, caught it off-guard. A white camelia which she had ordered a month before arrived on our doorstep too late, and shook me with inexplicable sobbing. And once, searching for something under my father's desk, I came upon her lost slipper, probably carried there by a collie, and the sight of its small, intimate emptiness rocked me like an earthquake. These interludes brought relief from the anaesthesia of mourning. Nothing I felt seemed commensurate with the belovedness of the dead.

Looking back, I can see that the grief I expected was already upon me, and that I did not recognise it. It had come in another form, and was eroding me inside, I don't know how. My last remembered feeling – a month after her death – was of a growing delicacy and depletion.

The sight of my parents' home, with its weathered gate, its sheltering trees, grows no sadder with my recovered memory. On the contrary, her death had previously left a vacuum which my imagination filled with confused possibilities. But now this haunting stops. The house seems to undergo a painful but natural completion, as if it were itself again, or hers.

I find my father drinking tea in the kitchen with a wholesome-looking local woman of my mother's age. He is confused and a little ashamed by her presence, but I feel no resentment; rather this attempt to fill the void my mother left, the desire to rediscover her vanished comfort, seems to me a melancholy tribute to her. The woman gets up and shakes my hand, too boisterously, and says she must be leaving. Her hair bounces round her cheeks in a steely bob. She has brought my father a bunch of yellow tulips.

After she goes he says awkwardly: 'She's a neighbour . . . a good sort of woman.'

I wonder how well he is surviving. I recall how for days after my mother's death he walked about in a robotic stupor, until I became afraid that the inner life had died out of him, as it dies out of a crustacean, leaving the shell intact. Then one morning I noticed him studying a magazine article – I assumed it would be about cancer or bereavement (or collies). But no, it was a foreign affairs item, which he was reading for its own sake. And I thought: he's going to be all right.

But now, when I enquire about him, his coughing starts up and his eyes avoid me. He says: 'I seem to have so little energy. I spend my time just . . . staying alive.' He gives his short, dry laugh. 'But there's the garden to think about. And the collies, of course.'

He is always calling and fondling them, whereas before he never touched them. The youngest two respond with subdued affection. The oldest stares back cynically from her basket, and does not stir. Among my new memories I recall accompanying them to a dog show, and how enthusiastically my mother stacked and paraded her favourites, while my father watched in support. Then she became tired, her face suddenly ashen, and her bewildered refrain 'I'm too young to feel this' now darkens into presentiment. Her dogs failed, and I see my father and her going over to congratulate the winner. She did this with reserve, convinced of her dogs' superiority. But my father, I remember, chatted with the victor and expatiated on the silkiness of the champion's coat. And I realised suddenly: of course, he's relieved that my mother lost. Because for a while her love for her collies will perhaps be redirected towards him.

When he realises that I remember her dying, he reaches across the kitchen table and grasps my hand. His eyes are moist and bright behind their glasses. 'You've caught up with her.' Then I see how painfully I had abandoned him to the loneliness of his memory. He sighs and smiles. In his eyes, I realise, I had subtly betrayed her, leaving her depleted in the only life certainly left to her, the memory of others. He asks: 'How much are you still missing then?'

'Only a year.' And I'm unsure even of this. Stray islands appear in it, I think. 'But I've got her back.'

Within a month she was bedridden. Under her questioning the doctor's recommendation for radiotherapy turned out to advocate nothing but a painful delay, and she refused it. She shrank to a scaffold of bones. She would lie for hours unmoving, listening to the radio, drugged out of pain. Her skin had withered to yellow paper where her eyes seemed dilated and unnaturally glittering. She was being sucked away from inside.

My father and I took turns at her bedside. It is inconceivable that those hours might have vanished from my memory. Often we just sat in silence, listening to her breathing, waiting. She had lived her life so openly that passing intimacies and requests, fragments of secret shame or private memory, scattered my watches only thinly, and instead it was I who ached to talk, to disclose myself, as if I were asking her blessing.

But once, early on, she said: 'I used to think it cowardly not to fight disease. I thought if this ever happened to me I'd fight it to the end. But now I don't know.' Her hand splayed over the sheet above her heart, as if she were monitoring its beat, and sensing the speed with which her strength was ebbing. 'Your father wants me to fight it. But I think it's gone beyond miracle-working. It's more dignified to accept.' She added softly: 'I don't want to blind myself. I want to be peaceful.'

I had never thought my mother beautiful, but now the disease was starting to resculpture her face, scooping its cheeks and opening out her eyes; and I glimpsed the girl with whom my father had fallen in love. I took her hand. I said: 'If you accept it, you'll feel in control.'

'Yes.' She smiled at me, grateful. 'I don't want to leave in a mess.'

'No . . . .' Then I heard myself whisper: 'What do you need from us, what can I tell you? Isn't there anything . . . ?' The question dwindled out in its strangeness.

But she said: 'I want you to get on with your life. Keep an eye on your father; don't let him move into some geriatric bungalow. And I don't want the dogs got rid of.' Her head turned on the pillow and looked up at me with her newly-brilliant eyes. 'And I think you should get married, find a decent girl. Somebody solid.'

I said: 'I've got Jaqueline.' I'd known her four months, but had rarely brought her home.

My mother smiled her new smile: toothy, weakened. 'She's a clever creature. But I don't feel I know her.' She sighed. 'I'm sorry I won't know her.'

Then a collie squirmed through the door and

thrust its nose into her palm. She addressed it whimsically: 'We don't like this waiting, do we? It's no good for anybody. Let's all hope it goes quickly.' She had developed a trick of speaking through the dogs to us when something was painful, and now she added: 'A month should be enough.'

I repeated feebly: 'A month?' She had never said this before.

But within two weeks her face and body had collapsed inward, her voice dwindled and her eyes had taken on a querulous, helpless look, quite foreign to her. She could no longer stand, and it was then, in the last week of her life, that I would sometimes carry her to the bathroom, stricken by her lightness, and my father would watch, believing still that my strength might course into her, and that I was willing her back to life. But when I lifted her she let out mews of complaint, as if she were too heavy, and in her wide, vacant eyes I saw appear the hatred of her condition, her humiliation, and how she longed to be free.

Then I wanted her to die: this precious travesty in my arms. I wanted not only an end to her indignity in her own eyes, but an end to the unrecognisable person she was becoming, transfigured by suffering into a frustrated old woman. She was no longer my mother. Yet maybe my father is right, and I still held out some fragile hope for her. I don't know. I give up trying to know who I was at that time. I was starting to slide into my own trouble.

My father says suddenly: 'Do you want to go up there?' He means the churchyard. And I think it will be a kind of restitution, and say Yes.

We meet nobody we know in the village, and

123

the path to the church is deserted. Past the weathered and lichened Victorian headstones, we come to where an avenue of holly trees leads to the cemetery's end. From a distance I see that already new graves surround hers: a year's-worth of dead. I'm afraid to read their names. The place is full of my childhood: family friends of shadowy memory, church dignitaries whom my boy's mind thought indestructible. Already they seem to belong to another age. We stand by my mother's grave as we must often have done before, but I cannot remember a month beyond her death. Her headstone stands glaring and new. The grass is growing there again. I feel a sick shock at the finality of her inscription: the dates too little time apart, her unfamiliar middle name. Gold and white chrysanthemums stand fresh in a vase.

My father says: 'I try to keep it nice.' He bends down to pick away fallen leaves. Out of his loneliness he has worded the epitaph with more passion than he ever expressed to her in life. My hand comes to rest on his shoulder. I feel an odd peace. She has gone through a second death and restoration in me, so that I feel as if I were in dialogue with her again, and that she is changing. It is very quiet here. No birdsong in the late afternoon. Just the familiar continuum of the church beyond the trees, with its Norman tower sailing a wonky weather-vane.

My father's hands are folded in front of him, as if he were at prayer. He doesn't look at me. But suddenly he says: 'You won't remember this, Eddy, but last time we were here you said something about black holes which I didn't understand. Something about time reversing. It's foolish, I know, but it took my fancy.'

I try to imagine what we might have discussed, but I do not know if the past year broke down our natural reticence. What have we said? In the few days after her death, afraid to break our trance of mourning, we took refuge in Christian platitudes. But later, I know, we must have delved into the old repertoire of agnostic hope: the consolations of the unbeliever, which exist not in certainties, but in the infinite possibility of the unknown.

'I don't know what I said, Father.'

'You said that black holes were the nearest thing to God we had left.'

'I must have meant they were unknowable.'

'You said they were ubiquitous – or that was the latest thinking. And yes, that inside them time and space were drastically bent by the force of gravity, so the old laws broke down and unknown ones were created.'

I keep my gaze on the ground. I do not know what store he sets by these dreams. One by one, with each point he makes, the fingers of his right hand unclasp to tap his left knuckle. It's his schoolmaster's habit. I begin: 'There are all sorts of theories about . . . .' Then I imagine the faint, pleasurable sound of my mother laughing: she always ridiculed us when we talked portentously. 'There's an idea that if someone could vanish inside a black hole, time would go into reverse for them.'

My father says: 'So the past can come again.'

'Well, nobody can believe time is an absolute any more.'

I know what he is thinking, what he wants for her. But I do not know what I want. A future, I think, not a past. My hand is still on his shoulder.

Then he smiles to himself: a self-mocking smile

which I recognise. He says: 'I've lost out on the latest in astronomy. And I never did understand Einstein. But tell me, if you can't trace these black holes optically, how do you know they exist?'

The cemetery gardener trudges by, carrying a bucket. I wonder what he thinks we are discussing. I say: 'The material falling into a black hole sends out X-ray signals, and they've been picked up. And sometimes a star can be detected orbiting something invisible, something of tremendous density, which is slowly destroying it. We call them dark companions.'

My father's fingers have retracted into his fist again. 'Can you believe these theories?'

'I don't know. Nobody knows. Some scientists propose that anything entering a black hole will re-emerge into a different universe through a kind of "wormhole" and perhaps travel backwards through time.'

I don't understand this myself. But it is a bizarre comfort, standing above my mother's rectangle of grass, to take refuge in all our ignorance. And now the strains of agnostic hope are tuning up again in both of us, and we start to exchange their consolations in muted voices, as if afraid that she might hear and mock us – that time is circular, that it can be opened like a book at any page, that we are perhaps only dreaming it. We have the grace to laugh a little, for her sake. But we both feel light-headed, I think, touched by a suppressed hysteria, and his arm arrives across my shoulders too, so it must look as if we're about to break into Greek folk-dance.

Perhaps this amnesia has shaken me more violently than I realise, but all at once I find myself hypnotised by the total inexplicability of my existence, like a blink in eternity on the only planet known to sustain life among presumed millions. It's like a stupefying fluke. Or perhaps it's a trick of memory, and I've forgotten its context. Maybe I pass through wormholes in and out of separate amnesias, and that's what existence is: eternal lives. Fleetingly I even feel that my mother doesn't matter, that nothing is real in the sense that I've perceived it. Perhaps she never lived except in my mind . . . .

I must stop this. This is how people go mad. I bend down and feel the grass coarse and real under my palms. I say out of the blue: 'Black holes may be anything, Father. Basically we're just trapped in our own heads. The Inuit – the Eskimos – thought the stars were seal-hunters who'd lost their way home.' Was it Jaqueline who said that? I feel a spasm of gratitude to her. So the possibilities never end. Nothing is perhaps what it seems. Even death, even hope.

My father says cheerfully: 'So we're each a kind of Eskimo, are we?'

My mother would have liked that. 'Certainly!'

We stand there a moment longer, then our hands slowly release each other and my father is adjusting his spectacles. I stare round at the graves, as if emerging from a trance. For four days I have been waiting to break into my own memory, yet for some reason I find all this unforgettingness around me heart-rending: the massed flowers, the tiny beds of pansies curved round the headstones.

It is now, insidiously, just as we start back along the path to the church, that I become aware of something beating up close beneath my thoughts. When I try to grasp it, it is like scrabbling for an object underwater, something soapy and amorphous. But it is untrue that memories always evade coercion, because after a minute of artificially putting it from my mind, I attend to it again, and it wells up into the day. It arrives not with the patina of most memories, dulled by constant recall, but with an intense, blinding clarity. It is trivial in itself, I know, but it emerges virgin and complete out of the past, like something alive, and stops me dead on the path. It is as if I'd only just lived it.

My mother is standing by a wall like this beside us, the same amber stone. Her body is firm and whole again. She is staring at a field where sheep and geese are grazing intermingled, and her girlish chin juts and quivers as she cries: 'Look at that! The whole lot muddled up!' It must be my father, standing off-stage, who murmurs something. She laughs back. 'When I was a child I remember a wood where pheasants and pigs bred together. The pigs quite clean in the wild. Wonderful.' And she goes on smiling over the wall, elated by the peaceful conflation of things. 'Look at the ram! . . . Look at the gander!'

I know this is only a buried image unaccountably delayed, but it comes with such immediacy that it seems to post-date her death. Her cheeks have fleshed out again, and the spring is back in her voice. She is touched by a puppyish excitement. It is as if for one vivid moment she responds to our doubts about the fixity of time, and decides to return. This is my foolishness, I know. But it strikes me with a heady confusion, and my reason is powerless to relocate the pleasure on her face as she praises the cleanliness of pigs.

13

It is long after dark when I return to the house, and Naomi's car is standing by the porch. I drive on towards the sea, the chalk track white under the moon, and walk for an hour along the cliffs. This malaise has started in me again, the sweating, the pulsing in my forehead, but I decide to walk it off. Beneath me I can hear the waves chopping at the base of the cliffs. I must have walked this way fifty times before, but it's still a blank. There is no sound but the breakers and the crunch of my steps. A diffused moonlight polishes the sea.

Now a cold wind has got up, and I turn my face to it. My mother's memory still shakes in me. I feel as if something in me may veer out of control. Beneath me the site of the wartime radar station is lost in its ruins, and night creatures are rustling under the vegetation that covers it. I climb to the headland and shelter in the lea of a rough-stoned edifice – some chapel or watch-tower – perched four-square above the point. Its door is open but I can make out nothing inside except a low vault and a rectangle of walls. Outside, the wind is sharpening.

As I return, the pressure inside me subsides, as if something had been reversed (but it hasn't). Rabbits scatter from my headlights down the drive, and the front windows of the house are all in darkness. I let myself in quietly. A light glows under the bedroom door. I go into the kitchen in the routine hope that something will awaken my memory, and sit on the table and think of nothing. This room is so richly made for living in that if my memory recovered it, I feel, it would bring a peculiar consolation and perspective. But instead, because I have sat here several times, it is coated in recent familiarity – I know the contents of all the apothecary bottles and little drawers – and it brings nothing.

I ease open the bedroom door so quietly she doesn't hear. She is sitting up in bed, reading. For the few seconds before she notices me I see her private face, shaped only by its own thoughts. It is softer, serious; but although I don't know why I ever thought her plain – she is quite slender, dark-eyed – I cannot imagine loving her. Caught by surprise, she looks up at me with momentary hope of my memory having returned, then instantly it dies, and she lays aside her book and says: 'How was it?'

I linger in the doorway a moment, then close it behind me. I must look doltish – I am moving stiffly, as if I have no body. But I remember that to her there is nothing odd that I am in our bedroom. I sit down on the end of the bed, as though I were visiting a patient. 'It was strange. Soon after I left you I remembered my mother's death.'

She stares at me in her exacting way, and says nothing. This look is, of course, a reticent kind of question; but I realise I cannot share this death with her. I hoard and savour memories now, even trivial ones: they are so hard-won, so elusive. I even feel physically stouter after recovering them, as if they were my body. I don't know why I should care much what she thinks – how little I know about her! – but I ask her: 'Do you believe in an afterlife?'

Sometimes, before replying, she leaves a silence, like a delicate, intervening thought, or the unnerving, split-second pause in exchanges via satellite telephone. Then she says: 'No, I think death is natural and reasonable. We ought to die. But then I'm an artist, even if you think I'm a rotten one, so I like change. It's my meat and drink.' As though she might have hurt me, she says: 'Grief is just for ourselves, isn't it? It's not for the dead. It's about our being separated. But the dead don't feel separated.' She's plucking at the duvet. 'Do I sound cold?'

'You sound reconciled.'

'Oh no I'm not! I'm alive!' she laughs. 'But you used to accuse me of being soulless.' This disclosure makes her wince. I think she regrets saying it; but it's too late now. 'You said my paintings frightened you, that I had a cold eye.'

I hear this with faint wonder. What else did I think of her? I get up from the bed, and hunt for my pyjamas in the chest of drawers, feeling nervous. I find myself riffling through her pullovers before I locate them. I start to undress, then go to the bathroom. I feel displaced, as if I were acting somebody else. For a long time I wash and shave at the basin, disquieted by my tense face, and clean my teeth meticulously, as if before making love. Then I stand staring at myself in the full-length mirror: I see a tall, wracked-looking man, comical in his pyjamas. If I were a woman I wouldn't touch me.

I hesitate by the door. I feel my heart light and scuttling. When I go in again she's picked up her book and continues reading while I climb into the far side of the bed. But the book quivers faintly in her hands. For a while I lie tense, my gaze roaming over the ceiling, the walls, listening to her turning the pages – but too quickly to be really reading. If this were not so terrible, it would be funny. Then I hear her put the book aside and her hand hovers at the lamp-switch. 'Do you want to sleep?'

'Not yet.' There must be something to say. Perhaps if Jaqueline did not exist, I would say to her: wait, wait until I'm well. After all, there must have been something I loved in her.

The silence elongates between us. The intimacy, the soft light, suggest painfully, confusingly, what I cannot feel. She is wearing a blue nightgown, lying with her face away from me.

I say: 'I'm sorry.' I put out a hand.

She squeezes it and withdraws. She asks: 'Can you tell what has made your memory return sometimes? Is it after you've been peaceful or angry or anything? Or because something reminded you?'

I wish I knew what would remind me. 'It just seems to happen.' I've looked for a common factor myself. 'The first time it came in a flood, it was wonderful. The second, almost casually. Then I remembered my mother looking into a field – an ordinary image – but it was like a revelation. I don't understand any of it. Sometimes I fish about in my mind, imagining I can catch something unawares, but it doesn't happen.' Why does she want to know this? 'Memory seems to return when I'm distracted altogether.'

She says: 'I've heard it's possible to recover memories under drugs. Has any doctor suggested that?'

'You want to dope me?'

She laughs. But I realise she's been reading about it, or consulting people. 'The trouble is, nobody seems to know anything.' Her sigh sounds frustrated, even a little angry. 'If it was me, I'd expect people's faces to remind me.' But she says this without bitterness – she's turned away. 'Or objects. Certain objects I'd loved.'

'But the emotional charge of something makes no difference.' I'm conscious of defending myself, although she hasn't accused me. 'Memories just return haphazard.'

I've gazed at objects too, hoping. In amnesia they become alien all around you. You can't tell if they have a history for you, a secret meaning. You look at them as at so many closed doors. You grow to distrust.

She says: 'I believe some people remember through touch' – but she's still turned away – 'or taste or smell. Years ago I remember the smell of coriander making me cry, and I had no idea why. Then I realised. It reminded me of cod liver oil, and of my grandfather – he died when I was seven – who used to coax me into taking it. Has a scent ever reminded you of anything, or a flavour? No?' Her voice lightens in surprise. 'Perhaps I should find you some rosemary or a madeleine tea-cake!'

I remember breathing in one of her scents the night I returned here, believing she was Jaqueline, and hoping that the faint, woody fragrance would recall her. The bottle is on my bedside table. But of course it summoned nobody. I say: 'I've tried that already, the night you weren't here.' I point to the bottle. 'But the genie had a day off.'

'So that's where it went!' She reaches across and takes it, her shoulder arched over mine. Her hair splashes my face – she doesn't notice – before she returns to her side and lies still. Then I feel a cold unreality, as if my situation were being borne in on me for the first time. I've violated her privacy. I lie beside her alone in this lamp-light, her hand protruding from her nightgown on the duvet beside me, and I feel nothing. It strikes me, irrationally, that it is strange of her to allow it. It is an act of touching trust, and it turns me shabby. I'm just a voyeur here. It is as if I've slipped in under a false identity, and that she hasn't noticed. I even catch myself thinking: could she become a friend? That's all I want of her. I want to wipe out all her subtle, beseeching looks, the fleeting expressions of disbelief, the glimmers of self-steeling when she is withholding herself. Because she still cannot believe that I won't suddenly say: 'Ah Naomi! Naomi!' and take her in my arms.

I know this is atrocious for her. I know. But I can't pretend. I don't know what more to say to her. Once, when half-turned to me, I sense her start to trace a gesture, something loving, habitual to us, but which she aborts almost before it begins.

We lie in silence for a minute. Then a bird calls outside, like someone tuning up a flute.

She says: 'That's our owl.'

I wait for it to call again, but it doesn't. 'Why is it ours?'

A spasm of pain crosses her face. 'I'll wait for your memory.' I don't know how to comfort her. Suddenly her voice breaks: 'Edward, don't you remember anything of us? Has it all . . . ? Nothing?'

Then it dawns on me that she may disbelieve me. She's probably read that certain amnesias can be mixtures of psychoses and conscious evasion, an escape from the intolerable, as the foxy house-man said. Case histories are full of people who escape their responsibilities like that. And she, I suppose, became my responsibility. But I have to say: 'No . . . I don't remember. I'm sorry.'

She's turned round to me now. Her eyes stare at me from the pillow. They're wet, bright. I say again: 'I'm sorry.' Then I feel: if only I can re-member this, this intimacy, the way her eyes look, close to mine – surely I must remember – every-thing will return. If I don't remember this, what will ever break through? I say: 'I've tried. I keep trying.' But I know she can't believe that I can lie so close, our arms touching, our faces a foot apart, and that still I do not recognise her, and I watch her disbelief turn to a kind of appalled resignation, and at last her hands reach out and caress my cheeks, but wonderingly, desolately, and her fingers wipe over my eyes as if trying to pull back a curtain.

She says: 'Of course you've tried, I know.'

'I keep thinking something more will break in. Just now I walked to the headland. I must have done it umpteen times before – the radar station, the chapel – is it a chapel? But nothing happens.'

Her tiny pause intervenes. 'It's a chapel.'

Then she comes into my arms, her face lowered against my chest. Her body brushes light against mine, but her fingers cling to my shoulders, and she starts to sob in deep, soundless spasms which rack her whole frame. Once I ask her softly what she is weeping for – I feel there is something specific – but the question loses itself in the freak-ish tragedy of us, and I don't repeat it, but hold her until her tears lighten, and she falls asleep with her head still touching my shoulder.

14

The town of Tomohon lay in a valley between two volcanoes. Its name, we were told, meant 'The Place where People Pray'. On one side rose the symmetrical cone of Lokon, on the other the thick, shattered spire of Mahawu. As long as anyone could remember, they had acted up like a volatile couple: when one overheated the other went quiet. They took their victims piecemeal, in random outbursts, but the plutonic soil which coated them was too fertile for the local peasants to have left alone.

From Tomohon a bus travelled to a village in the lea of Mahawu, and we got off into a scattered community of farmers. Jaqueline was elated and impatient. She did not care if it was safe or not. She wanted to circle the crater's lip, and look into the earth's intestines. I scarcely recognised myself here. I seemed to be following, mesmerised, in her footsteps. Before this, I had seen the volcanoes only of southern Italy, lifting in scenic peace beyond a gentle Mediterranean.

But Mahawu was different. It festered in virgin jungle. Every few years it killed someone. No observatory monitored its moods. But almost at once a man with a smattering of English appeared, and offered to guide us up. He was wry and hardy. His bandy legs made a perfect oval under him. When we asked him when the volcano had last erupted, he did not understand, only echoed: 'Err-upt?'

'When did it last blow up?' I splayed my fingers into the air.

'Soon!' He grinned. 'Very soon.'

At first we laboured up a track sunk between dark-soiled fields freshly turned for yams. Underfoot the bamboo trunks laid down to stabilise it had subsided in the mud of new rains, where bullock carts slumped to their axles. Jaqueline hitched up her dress and took to vaulting the quagmires. Her legs were soon coated in mud like brown socks. She kept looking up at the confused undulations of forest hills in front of us, trying to locate the crater mouth. But our view was blurred in trees.

At the last shanty on the track the guide stopped and said: 'My brother here. New married.'

The man stood with his wife under their ramshackle porch. They smiled. His features looked blunt and puffy with happiness. Her hair poured to her breast. She was pregnant. How they saw us I don't know: these lean, pared Westerners so mysteriously restless. But Jaqueline and I stood smiling back at them, our hands momentarily linked. Recently I had hinted to her that we buy a flat together, but she had always escaped me in jokes. Now I said: 'They, at least, have managed to cohabit!'

She let out a scoffing 'Hah!', but touched her head to mine. 'Look at those all-purpose smiles!'

We climbed on through enveloping jungle. Around us fig trees and rattans squirmed from the black soil, wreathed in creepers and dripping with parasite ferns. Once or twice the track opened onto groves of bamboo and soft grasses, then closed again. In the silence our shoulders brushed and stirred the trailing lianas, and a breeze set the undergrowth in shimmering commotion. Jaqueline stopped and sniffed the air. 'Sulphur,' she said. But I could not smell it. The wind came again and all around us the leaves trembled like overlapping scales. They rustled and suffocated one another. Once they parted to show the smooth flanks of Lokon ascending to our west, and once the jungled valleys opened up below, with a blue curve of sea.

The guide went in front, uttering weird, high-pitched cries which nobody answered. Several times he fell back to talk with me. 'In England,' he began, 'what do you and lady do?'

I pointed at the sky. 'We study stars. Astronomy.'

He looked pleased at this idea. He asked: 'Lady your wife?'

She was walking ahead of us with long, light steps. Her hair left bare her soft neck. I said: 'Yes, she's my wife,' and our union, as I spoke it, became possible, and brought a spurious gush of pride, so that I savoured us in his eyes.

Then the path steepened and a wave of sulphurous steam blew through the trees.

'Not good. Not good,' the man said. 'You go on?'

'Yes,' I said, and Jaqueline, overhearing, turned round and grinned. She began to stride ahead as if someone might change their mind, and a few minutes later, where the jungle thinned to a verge of grass above us, I saw her halt and stare down. The stench was nauseous now, and a miasma of smoke was rising behind her. She turned round and lifted her arms in the air. Her eyes were shining. 'This is *it*!'

I emerged beside her under the open sky, and stopped in astonishment. Within a few strides the earth had changed. The jungle luxuriance dwindled into an eerie fringe of pink-feathered grass, and beyond this, beneath our feet, the whole mountain summit broke open. The chasm must have measured quarter of a mile across, and its sides plunged almost sheer three hundred feet. There was something shocking about it. Without warning it had burst the earth like a colourless ulcer, and in its bowl a greenish lake was roaring with geysers. Above the crater wall the grass was burnt to black spikes and the rocks dimmed to an igneous glitter. And all around us, blurred by the sulphur-smoke, an amphitheatre of healthy mountains and valleys swam in their own cloud.

Jaqueline kissed me in triumph. 'I never expected it to be like this!'

The guide stared at her and turned away: in his culture nobody publicly kissed. She noticed him, and shrugged.

Beside us a section of the crater had broken in, so we could clamber down for a hundred feet. We might have been descending Gehenna. The ground had blackened to charred roots and half-incinerated stones. The heat blazed and refracted from the rocks. The colours of the scarps reduced to etiolated greys and russets. We could hear the geysers invisible below us, like distant waterfalls. Vertically above, the disc of the sun hung stifled in steam.

We reached the burnt lip of the final drop. On every side the slopes were starting to crack, and threatened to crash in. The guide said: 'We stop here.' He was fondling the cross on his necklace. 'Lake almost gone,' he said. 'When water gone,

Mahawu explode!'

So the lake was a safety-valve. It looked as evanescent as water in a frying-pan. Its edges were wavering flats of fissured rock, and its shallows pulsed and simmered in different zones of artificial green. I imagined the volcanic magma boiling an inch beneath its bed. I tried to photograph it through the smoke, but its detail, at this height, eluded the lens. Yet when the sun struck the far scarp, it shone in the viewfinder with an unearthly glamour, so that I photographed it five or six times, in disbelief that I had captured it.

Then the guide's hand was tapping my arm. 'Look, look.' He pointed along the crater's rim. 'Lady dangerous.'

Fifty yards away I saw Jaqueline walking along the edge of the crater. She already looked isolated. The guide's face was taut and hard. But at first it was only a light shiver of anxiety that made me follow her. I shouted at her to stop, but although she must have heard me she didn't turn round. The slope slithered into pumice and basaltic shale. I tried to run, but we were too close to the edge now and a skein of stones was sliding underfoot. She was walking with tense, buoyant strides, ignoring me. I bellowed: 'Jaqueline! It's unsafe!'

She turned once, as if at some irrelevant sound, and made a flipping motion with her hand. The smoke billowed up from below and almost hid her. Far beneath us, just above the water-line, a sulphurous yellow fissure was blasting steam over one end of the lake. I closed within ten yards of her. She was walking with nerveless intent. The cliffs plunged vertically under her, and little porous pebbles went skittering down from her feet. High on the slope above us, the guide was

running and calling frantically: 'Lady dangerous!
Hatti-hatti! Lady dangerous!'

I shouted again. She stopped and shot me a
smile, then called: 'Are you frightened?'

'Don't go on!' I didn't dare approach her nearer
in case I dislodged more debris. So I just stood
helpless ten yards from her, but a foot nearer
safety than she was, back from the abyss. She,
meanwhile, stared down at the yellow smear of
cliff and its belching geyser, elated by this terrible
core of earth, her hands on her hips. Rust-
coloured cinders and stones were oozing around
her toes and beneath her sandals, then slipping
loose and puttering into space. I thought: she
doesn't mind if she dies. She doesn't value herself
in the least. For a moment of heightened life she'd
throw it away.

Over those ten yards she teased: 'You're white
as a ghost. Stop worrying. This is wonderful!'

'Come back. Now.' I held out my hand. My
voice was half lost in the turmoil of noxious
smoke and the geysers raving below. My eyes
were smarting.

'I didn't think you'd try to join me.'

Then she turned and began to follow me back. I
could hear her harsh breathing. I blundered into
the shelter of the nearest gully and clasped her to
me, craving the solid flesh of her in my fingers, the
living woman. She said: 'I was okay!' She was
flushed and tingling with elation. But I was
shivering like a baby.

'What the hell were you doing? What got into
you?'

She ruffled my hair. 'I was just trying it. I
wanted to see if I could do it.' She wiped the sweat
from her face, but she sounded frivolous. 'It

141

wasn't that bad.'

'It damn well was.' I was grasping her angrily. 'And what about me? Were you trying to kill me too?'

'Your life isn't mine.'

'I know it's not.' But it is, in a way it is. Even now. 'Don't you think you're mortal? Or don't you give a damn?' I wondered then what on earth I was doing in this Godforsaken country, with its dark history and volcanic cankers.

'Oh I don't give a damn!' She kissed me, our lips gritty with dust. 'I'm your dark companion! And now that guide is coming, and if he doesn't fall in the lake he'll want to know what on earth . . . . Just tell him I'm a woman!'

After this, a balance in us changed. Its seed must have been there all the time, waiting for something to nourish it. Earlier it had not occurred to me that our feelings were unequal. If in our love-making she sometimes seemed to be dreaming her own voracious dream, I knew that it was I who awoke this in her – that I was the agent of her loving, if not always its object – and that had been enough for me, bewitched as I was by her vitality and irreverence, her mind's hunger, her body's beauty.

But now I sensed her sliding away. This may have been half illusion, I don't know, but soon in my talk and touching I detected a fatal tinge of supplication, an anxiety to please which had been unconscious before. She seemed no longer to entrust herself, nor to be deeply vulnerable. But then perhaps she never had been, and I had not discerned it. Overnight we had grown precarious.

I was conscious of my anger too: anger at my help-lessness. For above all I became tuned to a tor-menting delicacy. Her separateness became my obsession. This was the separateness which I had loved so whole-heartedly in her before – in the woman I had sometimes held away in order to admire. Now it chilled me.

Perhaps it was some intimation of my mother's death which sparked this fear of loss. I don't know. But by our last day's holiday I was haunted by the idea that we would never go away together again.

Somewhere we came upon a grove of tombs – sturdy megaliths as old as a thousand years – which had been assembled under the frangipani trees in a half-abandoned museum. We wandered them in ignorance. The region's early history was opaque to us, and seemed unknown even to its inhabitants. ('God ate our history,' said a woman darkly.)

The graves were like tall stone mushrooms, in whose stems the dead had been buried upright. The roof-shaped lids were carved with reliefs of their occupants. High grass lapped at their eaves. Inside, the bodies had sat clear of the ground, so that their rotting would not anger the earth-god. They looked indestructible. In some chambers whole families had been immured together, squat-ting on top of one another until their bones mingled. They stared out from their gables in stone indifference, with pursed mouths and button eyes. Most were naked; but some nineteenth-century sarcophagi showed figures sporting the hats and frock-coats of the European coloniser. They appeared to have passed unbroken from nudity to imitation.

Jaqueline patted them like children as she went

by. 'Here's a hunter . . . there's a farmer . . . .' They were defined by their professions: the dogs of the huntsman, the stance of a wrestler, the birth-pangs and delivery of a mother. Jaqueline stared at this childbirth in silence – a splayed doll ejecting a larval-looking baby – and I wondered what she was thinking. The relief celebrated so flagrantly a prospect she found disquieting, a maternal confi-dence in the arrival of an extra human being.

Nearby was the worn image of a couple. They stood four-square and blank-faced on their lid: the model – or illusion – of a happy marriage. We found ourselves looking at them side by side, just as we had looked at the newly-weds under the volcano. In stone, too, they seemed to find union simple; and we, still apart in our flesh, confronting them over the divide of time and race, could only imagine their world easier than our own. I touched my hand to her waist, and felt the faint, warming response of her hip.

She said: 'I wonder if those families enjoyed being buried on top of one another.'

I imagined they did. 'I think it's comforting.'

'Not to be buried on top of my mother!' She escaped my hand in an abrupt movement – per-haps unconscious – which pricked my heart. She was walking away. I thought: I can't go on like this, I must take hold of myself.

So we wandered separately among the stone chambers, while my frailty continued. Because today was our last, I ached to freeze it in some per-manent or retrievable form. Under the guise of photographing the more eccentric decoration on the tombs, I took pictures of her instead, but covertly (she disliked being photographed), so that sometimes I captured a preoccupied profile examining a carving, sometimes a startled face which thought it had got in the way. But suddenly the angles and moods of this face were infinite. She had become ungraspable. In this futile exercise, I know, I was driven by the pathetic passion permanently to hold her, to recapture what I imagined I had once owned. But I could no longer tell which was the hallucination: her closeness to me then, or her distance from me now. I only despised this possessiveness in me. I never admitted it to her, nor showed her the photographs.

And that night I deluded myself with her. She was tired, and slid away into her sealed world. But I wilfully forgot her desertion, and made love to her body as if this could redeem us, and slept with my head on her breast where the illusion of closeness depended only on her skin against my lips.

15

It's been five days now. Sometimes I feel that the pressure of forgetfulness is growing greater all the time, condensing the past blank year into an unyielding nugget. But within a few hours I will be overtaken by an inner fragility. Then I become afraid that a horde of memories may gatecrash me, and that I'll be riddled with images and knowledge lost out of context.

I walk along this sea because there is nothing else to do. I can't concentrate to read, or listen to music. And simply to wait is intolerable. So I look for something here – an angle of cliff, the flight-pattern of sea-birds – to startle me back into wholeness.

The ocean is almost waveless, as if I were back in Sulawesi. I go west along the cliff top where I can't remember walking before. It is so warm, so silent – the headlands pushing over the water in fingers of pure mist – that it becomes peacefully alien, dissociated from any past or present. The sea is just an inverted sky, sucking at the rocks. Far out, two yachts are inching over the glass. It is Naomi's country, of course: but its recovery would surely return all the past to me.

Yet nothing disturbs its suffocating peace. The sea goes on lisping at the shore. The sun falls down an empty sky. I search for something distinctive, something which will ask my memory a question which it can't confuse with any other question: a cliff-side memorial to dead marines, the flight of wood-pinioned steps which carries the path up a valley. I stare at the columns of rock teetering free from the mass of the cliff – smoothed like co-agulated cement, or split into wind-made bricks – which hang fire for a century or two before join-ing the debris below. But I watch these phenomena with shrinking hope, and when towards sunset I emerge above a horseshoe bay of symmetrical perfection, I imagine it evoking nothing but itself, curved beneath me in a self-contained arc of sand. Down there the waves make a noise like rustling tissue paper. Above them, in this emptying light, the grey cliffs are putty-smooth, and above them unfold velvet fields. Nothing means a thing. I might as well be looking at a picture, or less than this (since a picture could evoke a memory of itself) – at the computer graphic for a seaside holiday. The only movement is the running of a black dog – tiny from this height – along the crescent of the bay.

At dusk I go back to the headland where I walked last night. Its chapel is pitched like a pagan tent on the cliff top: an enigma in lichened stone. Its roof – I see now – rises to a stone cross, and rough piers buttress its walls against sea-winds. I peer into a chamber fetid with damp. It is lit by a single lancet. A massive central pillar upholds the vaults, and a font is splashed with bird-droppings. Something earthy and primitive pervades the place, from before the birth of Christianity. It is not aligned with the east, and its altar is thrust diagonally across one corner. But it doesn't stir a single memory.

I return to the cottage and pour myself some

Scotch and put on CDs which I'm too restless to listen to. Naomi, luckily, is away on an assignment, and won't be back until late. But I don't know what to do. The news on her miniature television makes me think that nothing has changed. Then I wonder if anything I have bought in the past year gives a clue to my recent preoccupations. Among my CDs I find some jazz and a Beethoven string quartet, which are new. I listen to them lethargically. When the cavatina from the quartet arrives I imagine for a moment that I remember it; but the thought and the melody fade together – just an illusion – leaving me with the notion only that I may have listened to this with Jaqueline, or that it embodied some thought of her: a flowering and scattering of notes so strenuously beautiful that I turn them off before they end.

In my study I had not thought to investigate what obsessions my newly-bought books might betray. For all I know I had become fascinated by lacquerware or ornithology. But I find nothing unusual. The only surprising volume is a second-hand edition of Yevtushenko poems. I open it, looking for somebody's name, but it is uninscribed. It parts automatically on a much-fingered poem which I recognise only in my over-heated imagination.

> *I am conscious that these minutes are short*
> *and that the colours in my eyes will vanish*
> *when your face sets.*

The words make my eyes prickle. I've become dangerously suggestible. Soon I may start to invent memories, and come to believe them. I associate these emotions with my mother. Now that she is dead I am conscious of her nature in me as I was not before, and cherish it, because it is all that is left of her. In some way it seems to absolve me too. I belong not only with myself: I am my ancestry, the result of others.

So I recognise my disgust, too, when I find the lightest pencil sketch of myself (I'm sure it is me) in Naomi's studio. She is planning to paint me again, like some specimen in her personal laboratory. The sketch is a fragment: a reference or an idea. Its face remains a virtual blank, but the figure is seated, I think, in the orangery chair. Why has it no features, I wonder? What the hell is she waiting for? For me to come alive to her? There is something gross and judgemental about the process. It's like an empty report sheet. Yet in this fragility I get the ugly feeling that she knows me better than I do, that whatever she paints, I shall become. I could grow to hate her.

Towards midnight I go to bed, leaving the lamp and the radio on. My mind falls vacant. I turn down the noise until it sounds far away. I must have dozed off, because after an hour, it seems, I hear water splashing in the bathroom, and see her clothes in a small pile on the chair beyond the bed.

With that familiarity which is at once so natural and so strange, she enters the room in her nightgown and sits down at the dressing-table without noticing that I am awake. I watch her face in the mirror. She shakes her hair from its band and starts to comb it out. It is glossy, almost black. She wears her solemn, intent look. The sleeves of her nightgown fall down from soft-looking arms. I feel that I should not be watching this; it carries a furtive eroticism. Yet I go on observing her eyes in the glass, which I expect at any moment to catch mine.

In the end I say: 'I'm awake.'

'I know.'

'Nothing happened today.'

'I'm sorry.' She smothers whatever disappointment she's feeling. She goes on brushing her hair. She says: 'You've already recovered so much. The rest will come.'

I feel I should ask: 'And what about you? Who were you dissecting today?'

If she senses resentment, she does not betray it. 'A London solicitor. His wife chose me to do his portrait, I'm not sure why.'

'Perhaps he's smug and she wants him disconcerted.'

She chooses to smile in the glass. She gets up, adjusts her nightgown at her shoulders, and goes round to her bedside table. Then, as she climbs in beside me, I despise her, as if she were prostituting herself. She stretches out under the duvet, looking at the ceiling, and her hand lies near mine. Its fingers are uncurled – as if in invitation – and although I know that this is a natural way for a hand to lie, I can't suppress my contempt. I wonder why I did not feel this last night, and can only imagine that it is because last night I climbed into bed after her.

But almost at once an unnerving excitement at her novelty overtakes me. Her hand now seems inert, but suddenly its inertia is frustrating. What's happening to me? I turn a little away from her. I think: somehow this is soiling both of us. I'm trying to distance her when I say: 'I see you're starting another portrait of me.'

'I wanted to, but I can't.'

'What stopped you?' I feel perversely disappointed. 'Is my face so strange?'

She says: 'No, not your face.'

'But you left it blank.' I sound bitter. 'Don't you feel I exist unless I remember you?'

'If I paint you now, it seems to make your condition permanent.'

'You're superstitious.'

'No, I just can't do it.' She sounds puzzled, unable to explain. Perhaps, after all, she doesn't want to hurt me.

'Don't you feel you're using people sometimes?'

'That's hard.' Her head turns towards mine. 'You know, when Monet was at his wife's deathbed – he adored her – he still couldn't help noting the colours of her skin. He was horrified at himself, and I understand that. I don't know how you escape it.' Her hand alights on the duvet above my thigh. 'Did that sketch upset you?'

'Only a bit.' But the presence of her hand has started up this spasm of need. I half twist towards her. She sees my face and her own indefinably changes. Her fingers start to exert a gentle grip.

'You shouldn't be upset. I know it seems callous, but in painting I have to give . . . a particular kind of attention.' The pressure of her hand is inescapable now. Her voice has blurred. She is starting to play a game, and I am playing it too, responding, and neither of us yet acknowledging it. She says: 'Maybe it's true that artists have a splinter of ice in the heart.'

But her face contradicts her, at least for now. It is softly sculptural. I say: 'Doesn't affection tinge your paintings at all?' I remember her unrelenting portrait of me.

'I try to make it not. I try to see without attachment, without anything. I try to remove myself. It may be that I'm harder on someone I love.' But her words are a kind of love-making. My hand is holding her wrist now, and for a moment she is uncertain, I think, if I mean to restrain or encourage her. Our legs are touching under the duvet. Fleetingly I think: how extraordinary. I had imagined that if ever I were to find her attractive, it would happen through remembrance. Yet the next moment I am gathering her, forgotten, in my arms, as if I were repeating some action endemic to me before, inevitable to my body at the touch of a particular hand.

My words fade. 'That's very austere . . . .' Then, with a helpless naturalness, my lips close on hers, and I glimpse her face dazed, its mask splitting apart, all the hope and longing flooding back. She enters my arms with a little start of hesitancy, perhaps unsure precisely whose embrace she is accepting. Then I feel her warm lightness against me. I imagine that my hands on her back and the suppleness of her shoulders must ignite some recognition, but they do not; instead I am overswept by pure, impersonal desire. Her body is hot and pliant: new. Yet she seems to creep so easily into the recesses of my own body, her lips finding a resting-place in my neck above the collar-bone, her fingers dug into my shoulder-blades, that I sense her familiarity with me in every movement, and it is oddly comforting, and seems to weld us with no effort of my own. At first she appears at peace with me, enclosed in the illusion of my old self. But deep inside her, from somewhere consciously suppressed, I can feel her shake with a tiny, intimate trembling, and her cheeks are wet – this woman I accused of coldness – and twice her gaze sweeps over mine in sudden hope that she will find recognition there, before her eyes close again.

152

I remember nothing. But I'm aware that this is part of the perverse strangeness and beauty of it. We have built up a trust, yet she comes to me with the frisson of a stranger. I can't help crediting her with a crazed faith. The shapes of her breasts and legs remind me of nobody's I have touched. Yet I feel as if my hands and skin are responding to hers with an instinctive knowledge, and that our needs have grown together in collusion, unconscious, so that my circling caress of her nipples or my touch between her legs were intuitively decided by us both over months of forgotten love-making, and have become my body's remembrance of her, which cannot be unlearnt. The nightdress has slipped below her ankles. No anxiety intrudes as I enter the illusion of homecoming, which pulses around me in its own fever. Her face is locked in my hands.

Later, lying in the dark, her hand still hot in mine, I try to sleep. Her breathing is inaudible, but occasionally she swallows, so I know she's still awake, and I imagine her eyes staring at the ceiling. A wind shifts the curtains, and rustles the oak branches outside the window. I cannot date the last time I remember lying like this: a year ago, perhaps, with Jaqueline in her flat near the observatory, she curled away from me. The memory is achingly clear, although not new. Then I wonder what I am doing beside this woman I do not know. I don't understand myself. I must have slept with her many times since Jaqueline, so why does one more make a difference? Yet it does, it does. I feel suddenly sick as the memories of Jaqueline start up again, and I don't even know where she is.

Naomi whispers: 'Are you all right?'

153

'I'm thinking.' Her eyes are open now, I'm sure, and she's waiting. Her hand is still in mine. I move roughly in the bed to excuse my relinquishing it. 'When did I say I loved you? Long ago?'

'Five months ago.' Her tone is level, cooled. I sense her retiring into herself. 'I know you may not say it again.'

'I don't know.'

'You can't know.'

In the dark our voices take on a disembodied clarity, their words at once more important and more abstract. I wonder: did Jaqueline leave me – or did I leave her – in some kind of panic? For a while I lie with this intangible event, and then – it is easier in the night – I ask: 'What triggered my breakdown, Naomi? Tell me. Was it my parting from Jaqueline?'

'Yes. But I didn't know you very well while you were with her. You seemed all right for a long time afterwards. We were happy.' The words take on a lapidary sadness in the dark. 'Then you suffered a kind of . . . delayed reaction.'

Why, I wonder? I can hardly imagine this. She must have exerted a terrible power over me. Then I ask: 'Where is she?'

She leaves her pause. 'I don't know where she is.'

I have given up thinking Naomi is jealous, but mention of Jaqueline turns her guarded and remote. I suppose my breakdown humiliated her. She says: 'Only your memory will explain it to you.'

But what if my memory doesn't return? I'll be condemned to this tumour inside me, unresolved. Then I'll have to go to Jaqueline as if I were an idiot with half a mind, and hope that she exorcises it. Jaqueline, so contemptuous of weakness! I can only go to her whole.

I imagine this with self-indulgent longing. Yet its prospect seems remoter than it did, I don't know why. I might be day-dreaming. Perhaps it is Naomi, her physical reality beside me, who is responsible for this dimming. She stirs slightly, as if settling into sleep.

I need to say something to her, something hard, but the words come out with foolish simplicity: 'I'm sorry I've been angry with you. It's not your fault, it's mine. You've been good to me.' But really I'm saying: I'm sad that I shall leave you, I know it's not just.

Perhaps it is my illusion, but I almost think she understands, because she says: 'You're thinking about Jaqueline.' Her voice contains the artist's splinter of ice. It's uncanny how she senses things, or knows me. We must have been close in our way. She says: 'Stay with me until your memory returns.'

It's like a threat. I say: 'It may never return.'

Her laughter comes muffled from the duvet. 'Then you'll be stuck here!'

This teasing eases my guilt. After a while her breathing sounds in light, regular sighs, and I think she is asleep. Outside, the branches thrash against the window-panes, and a light rain begins. For a little longer I lie confusedly awake, afraid that I won't sleep again. But this turmoil is ungraspable. I become the conduit for random thoughts which glide into one another. The next time the wind springs up I hear it only dully, as the accompaniment to a dream. After that I must have slept.

I wake up in the morning to find myself

shivering. Naomi has pulled the duvet round her in a chrysalis, and left me naked. For a minute I lie there, poised between irritation and amusement. Then I become conscious of something different: a deep, heavy reverberation which has been throbbing through my dreams for seeming hours. It comes – I realise now – from the Purbeck stone quarries two miles away, and although it's unconnected with anything detectable in my past, it is while I lie listening to it that I realise with cold excitement that my memories are returning.

16

The image on the screen was a bracelet of green-ish gold: the wreck of the Sanduleak supergiant in the Large Magellanic Cloud. Already the outer rush of its debris was slowing down as it ploughed into the gas-halo which had accumulated around it during its million-year decline; and when Jaqueline screened up earlier images to compare them, even I could detect a thickening brightness along the inner edge of the ring. Then she placed a window over various sections and magnified them, to show clear zones of expanded light.

She looked as I first remembered her, her concentration vivid and total. I felt there was nothing which the slanted eyes could miss. My hands came to rest on her shoulders, where she did not acknowledge them. She said: 'There was a change in the light. Quite suddenly. It came with the latest pictures from the Hubble. It looks as if a vanguard of debris – very uneven – is heating up the ring.'

She screened up an estimated light-curve whose magnitudes she was already revising, then a succession of figures which she was too excited fully to explain. Everything was speeding up. She foresaw the collision reaching its climax in less than ten months, and it had implications, of course, far beyond the firework of its impact. She had theories on the effect of stellar winds in the last millennium of a star's life, on the density of the surrounding atmosphere, on the variable presence of helium atoms and nitrogen. She was studying the chemical rearrangements which humans called stellar death.

But I was looking, ashamed, at how the tan from the Sulawesi sun still glowed light on her neck and hands, like an old memory. Nowadays that fierce intensity which I had so loved in her disquieted me. Once I had imagined its energy travelling a path parallel to my own; but now it seemed to point her indefinably away. I was becoming bitter with it, in a way I despised. While she was charting the effects of the greatest cosmic explosion in four centuries, I was watching the veins on the backs of her hands, and longing for her to touch mine on her shoulder. It turned me small and sentimental. I was becoming someone I did not recognise. I had even grown jealous of her supervisor, Hulton, whom she admired.

At last she said: 'Let's go to the tea-room.'

The tea-room was the forum for news and gossip between the disciplines, where the departmental galaxies and nebulae conferred with one another over a shambles of cutlery and the sipping of weak coffee. We found it almost full, and rumbling with news. One of the graduate students hurried across to tell us that Portway, the most time-serving of the academics, whom Jaqueline christened 'Harrumph', had just discovered a nova.

Jaqueline looked quite angry. 'How repulsive!'

But the man himself was amongst us – a smooth-faced mandarin, incandescent with smugness. He was walking shamelessly from table to table, distributing grey-scale images of the nova in two stages of its outburst. He had found it by luck during routine observations of a star-cluster in Draco. But he had lost any sense of disparity between himself and his achievement. He had already posted his bulletin with the International Astronomical Union, and was planning a series of articles. We research students were beneath his notice, of course, but he moved between the factions of Wertheim and Agate as if his feat would reconcile them.

Jaqueline was furious. It offended her stringent sense of justice. 'I suppose he hopes it'll be named after him, Nova Draco Portway, or something. Isn't it typical it should happen to Harrumph, instead of to Wertheim or Hulton? He's going now, thank God. Will he deign to smile at us . . . ? No.'

Portway passed unseeing through the doorway, panoplied in self-belief, and others began to drift away after him, murmuring, frowning, smirking. I could not be angry as Jaqueline was, only irritated. The discovery was so flagrantly serendipitous that it reflected nothing on its discoverer other than his vanity.

After a while we found ourselves alone in the room, toying with our tea-cups. In the lengthening silence I realised that I was growing afraid of her. It was four days since we had been together. I had left them vacant purposely, but she had made no move to fill them, and I had spent the evenings alone in my flat, restless, wondering. Now I found with astonishment that I could not bring the tea-cup to my lips because of my trembling. I took her hand. For a second it remained inert under mine, but then, as if she had just remembered me, its answering grip engulfed me with an idiotic surge of relief. She said: 'And what about your work? Has the request gone off?'

'Yes.' My voice sounded resentful, despite myself. 'Three days ago.'

Three days, and you never asked.

She just said: 'Good.'

But the request, in its way, was the culmination of my research, and she knew this. I needed her support now. After more than a year I had computed the black hole in Lepus at 4.7 solar masses, and our director's office had passed a request to Palomar Observatory in California for an optical image of the zone where it would lie. It was routine procedure, but nerve-racking. I hoped, of course, to see in that zone no star at all: just the void where a black hole might be. But the intricate edifice of my calculations all at once seemed fragile. How could anyone know what was happening in a zone so distant that the light which reached Earth had set out in the Palaeolithic age?

Jaqueline was still playing with her teaspoon. She looked dissatisfied. It was as if her anger with Portway were spilling over onto me. She said: 'It's odd, when you come to think of it, that you have to calculate from an arbitrary angle of orbit. I know it's inevitable, but . . . .'

I thought: hell, at this moment she questions my following a basic axiom, the only one possible. No word of encouragement. She can't even say 'Good luck'. She's my lover, my closest friend, but she sits there fiddling with her teaspoon and undermining my hypothesis, where even my supervisor had sounded cautious optimism.

She turned and grinned at me with a pretence of mischief, but there was no comfort in her smile. Her fingers snaked through her hair. She started to go back over old problems, citing mistakes incurred by other observatories, and where once I saw these as warnings against disappointment, they now struck me as a cynical distrust of success. Even her laughter stuttered out like a jamming machine-gun. She complained about the telescope observation periods, how dangerously short they were – the data so faint in a binary system as far away as mine. She returned to my outdated fear that the star was beneath the minimum mass for a black hole, and queried my diagnosis of its X-ray signature, stirring an old panic about burster signals which had negated my first computations. I lapsed into silence. I had no idea why she was doing this. Perhaps she did not know. I had always anticipated this moment as one of celebration. Only two months ago she would have radiated enthusiasm. Now she had gone dead on me, as if not my project but I myself – whatever it was that had drawn or challenged her – was no longer of interest. I don't know what my expression would have conveyed if she had turned towards me – a mixture of bewilderment, adoration and panic, I think – but I brushed back the hair from the nape of her neck and kissed it, and said: 'That's enough playing.'

And was it only playing, after all? Was I being hypersensitive? I said: 'Let's celebrate your project tonight, and mine. We'll have our own party. I'll bring . . . .'

'I can't tonight.' But she was smiling at me with her old radiance: the tilted eyes harpooning mine like fish. 'I have to go to a party in Bristol. But soon, perhaps tomorrow.'

It was from this time that I began to doubt my own judgement. My interpretation of Jaqueline's words and gestures became a neurotic obsession. Maybe I imagined half the changes in her. Perhaps my mother's death had shaken me deeper than I understood. But it was as if the germs of my need and her indifference, tiny at first, were fattening fatally off one another in a cycle which I could delay but not prevent. I tried to conceal my fear from her. But my smiles were like plasters across my face and my voice seemed someone else's. I had the impression that in some way she had mastered me, had devoured me with the same speed as she did books, politics, cosmic phenomena, had absorbed the worship she needed, then grown tired and was pushing on.

That evening, wandering about my flat, I thought how a few weeks earlier I had only to pick up the telephone or take her hand to feel her answering warmth. It seemed a century ago. Now the voice which had grown guarded, the body less touchable, made me sick with apprehension; and all the time she became perversely more precious. She seemed to have slipped away before I was even conscious of holding her, while I imagined it would last for ever. In my flat the things which she had given me – a sheepskin rug, two wooden bowls, a fossilised fish – were no longer natural to the place, but looked orphaned.

I tried to work, but couldn't. That morning I had bought some roses and phlox for her, and left them wilting beside my display unit, then carried them home. Now I could not bear their presence, and decided to take them to her flat. It was something to do. I wrapped their stems in damp tissue paper and attached a love-note. I felt adolescent. Driving through the darkening lanes, I wondered whose party she was attending in Bristol, and whether I might not have joined her. But to-morrow, I told myself, tomorrow will be different. And suddenly it was a source of wonder that I might feel her skin on mine again, and she be smiling, that the delirium would return of us folded against one another, the heat of her breast. This time I'll imagine it is our last love-making, I thought, cherish it, remember.

I parked in the village street and went down the lane to her flat. The summer evening was thickening into dark, and there was nobody about. It started to drizzle. At first a bend in the alley hid her windows from me. Then, one by one, they came into view, and I saw that there was light in them. It shone soft behind the curtains of her sitting-room. For a few seconds I stood numbly in the lane while the rain hardened. My heart began hammering me into faintness. Then I thought: of course, she's left the lights on to deter burglars.

I advanced across the lawn, still uncertain, and stood the flowers against her door. Faint from inside, I heard music. I stood for a minute under the porch, while the wretchedness settled inside me. The rain was hissing in the trees. I thought I heard guttural tones, coughing, muffled laughter, but could be certain of none. Then I padded round to the bedroom window, and found it dark. The windows above were dark too, of the harmless psychopath who collected things. I steadied myself against the wall. I imagined my way through a list of men she might be seeing, but arrived at no one. Several cars were parked beside hers in the lane, but they could have belonged to anybody. I returned helplessly to the lit windows. I was shaking. The curtains were drawn too close to disclose anything.

Undecided, I picked up the flowers from the door, and dashed the rain out of my hair. If I'm sensible, I thought, I'll go away and never mention this. Then I rang the bell. The door, I knew, gave straight onto the sitting-room, and the moment it swung back I would know. For an instant I pictured myself: a sodden schoolboy, clutching a bouquet. I must look pathetic. I straightened my shoulders and planted my legs apart, as if to withstand a gale.

The door opened. Beyond her was nobody: just some notebooks spilling off the desk where she'd been working, and the radio playing in one corner. I was overswept by relief. For an instant she looked baffled, then a spasm of irritation crossed her, and at last she succumbed to an undertone of cynical amusement. It was as if she were trying out these responses until she alighted on the most useful. She said: 'Were you playing detective?'

'No. I was planning to leave these flowers here. I thought you were in Bristol.'

She didn't answer, only stepped aside to let me in. I stood foolishly, angrily, in the centre of the room. My relief had vanished in a bleak bitterness. Rather than see me, she had preferred solitude. It seemed, in its way, more hurtful, more ominous, than duplicity with a man. I knew that I should simply have kissed her, handed her the flowers, and gone home. But instead I demanded: 'Why did you lie to me?'

'I was lying to be kind.' She laughed. 'You know how I find that difficult!'

'Why couldn't you tell me you just wanted the evening alone? I'd have understood that.' But I knew how I'd resented her recent silences.

'What's happened to you?'

'Nothing's happened.' Her tone was edged with irony. She sat down on the sofa and patted the next-door cushion for me as if I were a puppy; but she said: 'If you can't take my moods, I can't change them. I don't belong to you.'

I stayed glaring down at her. 'Is this just a mood?' I felt I was committing suicide, but I couldn't stop. 'Do I seem different to you, Jaqueline? Is it something in me?' All the pent-up anxiety of the past weeks was filling my lungs. 'You've just spat me out!'

'If you don't stop shouting the maniac upstairs will come down and add us to his collection.'

'I'm not shouting.'

'You're not making sense, Edward. I'm just myself, that's all.' She said 'myself' with an inflection of levity, as if this self were insubstantial. 'Relationships change. Maybe ours has. I don't know.'

I crouched beside her. She had gone pale with the English summer, her hair swept back from a face of stony calm. 'Why should we change, Jaqueline? If I haven't, and you haven't? You're the same in yourself, aren't you?' Her eyes reduced me to a familiar helplessness. 'You're the person I fell in love with. You have the same intelligence, beauty, everything.'

'It's a pretty picture.'

She said this so flippantly I couldn't bear it. It dismissed her worth and my love together. 'Don't my feelings mean anything to you?' I was furious at how I sounded.

She leant forward and patted my cheek as if I were a child. 'Of course they do.'

I held her hand to my lips. She said: 'But I won't

be blackmailed by "love". If I want to see you, I'll see you. If our needs are different, I can't help it.'

I said: 'The one who feels less always has the power.'

She smiled with the cynicism I hated. 'But suffering manipulates.'

I thought: she says that only because she can't suffer. She doesn't understand suffering. Since adolescence she's ruled out all leaning on others (she said so herself). I don't call that independence but emotional cowardice. Whatever it is, I know, neither of us can change it. I once felt my passion must uncover some new softness or trust in her; but it hasn't done so, and now it never will. Maybe I'm sentimental to want it, I don't know. I've given up knowing anything.

I was still crouched in front of her, my hands on her knees, as if I were comforting her, when I heard myself, stupidly, say the words impossible to her: 'I love you.'

She gave a shrug. It was only a tiny movement, but terrible. In its little compass it seemed to reduce our past and present to an incomprehensible error, and to close off any future. Suddenly I wondered if at some buried level she felt unworthy of being loved – her childhood had told her this – and so she had come to despise me.

But she was laughing, of course. 'Love, love! You go on as if it was nirvana, instead of a kind of sexual silliness. You've lost your sense of humour, Edward, that's what's changed in you!'

I could not tell how serious she was. It was enough for me that she was serious at all. I was stripping myself bare, like a fool. I knew that no woman – she least of all – would esteem a man who pressed his feelings so abjectly. But I still demanded: 'Do you despise me for loving you?'

Her laughter stopped under a momentary frown. Her lips compressed. She only said: 'I think your feelings reflect your nature, not mine.'

I stood up, my shoulders leaden. My depression was so heavy that I felt unsure if I could move across the room. The flowers were on the carpet beside me, and I collected them mechanically. She looked at me with a relenting smile. 'Do you want to stay? You can if you like.'

I surprised myself by saying: 'Not tonight. Perhaps tomorrow. I didn't expect to see you' – the words were shorn of accusation. 'I'd better go.' I patted her cheek as she had done mine.

It was only after the door closed on me that I realised I was still holding the flowers. I must have looked a half-wit. For a moment I wanted to throw them into the bushes, but I laid them back against her door.

It seemed such a small thing: a white lie, and some passing cynicism. But I remember nothing that ensued to redeem it. If our estrangement had arisen from some specific cause, I felt I would have cured it. But instead I had simply faded in her eyes; I was no longer new, and she had overrun me. In the observatory, while I awaited my results from Palomar, I became self-doubting and distracted. Through the glass door to her department I could glimpse her bent head any time I wanted, the lights in her hair like a fractured halo, and sometimes I went in with a pretence of casualness to keep track of her work.

It was only by fluke that I once arrived as her superior left. He was a handsome man, already

167

greying in his forties, and his urbanity slightly repelled me. I heard him say: '. . . So your angstrom figures for carbon are inadmissible. Look back at the IUE spectrum.' Then he brushed past me, looking peeved.

I came and stood behind her. Her face was buried in her hands. I heard her whisper: 'Oh God.' Her visual display unit was crossed by a graph of predicted magnitudes for her supernova. I put a hand on her shoulder and her own came up and grasped mine without her looking round. Then I felt a shameful burst of relief at her wretchedness, because it was drawing us closer together. I asked: 'What happened?'

Her voice was shaky. I'd never heard her like this. 'I don't think I'm up to it.' Her breathing came in sharp, panicky sighs.

I kissed her. She still did not look at me. I said: 'You are, you know you are. It can't always go perfectly.'

Her head jerked upright and she shook it as if shaking off tears, but her eyes were dry. 'How the hell could I do that?' She was trembling between anger and alarm. 'Just leave out a whole fucking equation! I get all the detail right, then I miss what's staring me in the face.'

'Everybody does it, Jaqueline. *Everybody*.'

'I can't afford to do it.'

'What do you mean?'

'I just can't afford to.' For the first time, she looked at me, and I saw that her features, once inseparable from confidence, had dislocated into a tense despair. I felt a shock of surprise. Her mouth was depressed in a girlish pucker, as if before crying. I smoothed my hands over her face, willing it to calm. I thought how often in the past few days

I had wanted to break its self-sufficient mask, and now that it was broken I felt dismayed.

She said: 'This has set me back days. I know there's someone doing similar work at La Silla, but Hulton refuses to put me in contact with him.' She wiped the image from the screen. 'I'm just a research student. And now I'm making mistakes like some half-witted undergraduate.'

'So have I. And so, you can bet, have Wertheim and Hulton and all the others.'

'Not like this, not like this.' She dashed away my hand. 'What the hell do you do?'

'You just carry on and it comes right.'

'Does it?'

'Yes. In a few weeks it won't even seem important.'

She said bleakly: 'It will.' She gave a havering sigh. 'You'd better get back to your office.'

I stood up and touched her cheek. She looked at me unreadably, then said 'Thanks', and in an odd, abrupt gesture twisted her mouth and kissed my hand.

17

Memory stops here, or dwindles into trivia. And each time it ends, I think that no more will return. So the end of us will be this, her awkward kiss, like a premonition. And always the last memory stops at a hallucinatory crossroads, where there still seems to be choice, although I know everything is already past. But this is where I wait.

The memories seem more invasive now. They percolate in unnoticed, as if I've grown porous. And the idea never leaves me that in an hour, or a minute, I may realise something new, something worse, as if I were plummeting into a vortex of past images, orbiting in their own time-scale. Still I have the childish hope that I can cure us of the disease which must already have destroyed us, because I'll come to her innocent out of our past. It's like asking someone to join you in a dream. And then I imagine her eyes hard on me, hear her laughter.

It's corrosive to be frightened of the one you love. You dwindle away. But I'm more afraid of her absence. That's what she's reduced me to. That's what I've permitted. I can't be here, away from her, much longer. The booming of the quarries continues in my head long after they've gone silent. Naomi moves quietly to her studio, and in the afternoon I tell her I'll be gone for a while. I'm torturing her under her smile. I wonder what she's painting.

I get into the car and tell myself I don't know where I'm driving. But I know, I know. The roads uncoil out of my new life and into my old one. At first there are only small changes in the quilt of the fields, the contour of the hills. But after an hour I know the lanes by heart, and the illumined dish of the observatory lifts into view under a starless evening. I feel as I might passing my old school, somewhere I inhabited long ago, in another life, and it sucks me back with a little shiver of unease.

What can I say to her? That I exist in an earlier time, that to me we are still lovers? What could that be to her? Yet to her I've been absent just two weeks. I can't imagine this. To me she's been absent half my life. She'll say: 'Oh hi, Edward. I hope you've had a good rest?' and look at me with the eyes which I used to imagine saw everything.

And what do I say? 'I'm sorry, I have amnesia. I live in a dream of us. Meet me there.'

I don't want to hear her laughter.

I've lost less than nine months now, and even in these stray images appear, as though my brain were lighting up in isolated windows. But if crueller memories break through, even in these few miles which separate us, I think I'll turn back. Because I can recover her only with the courage of ignorance. I need this forgetfulness.

I park in the village street, as I did often before. A few men are drifting in and out of the pub. For a while I stay in the car's warmth, steadying my heart, my hands. I try to rub colour into my cheeks. It drains away. I think up lucid explanations of myself, austere, simple facts which will not alarm her. When I climb out of the car, the air is cold.

Then I hear: 'Edward!'

A stout young man in a brown suit is hailing me from the pub door. I have no idea who he is. He advances and clasps my hand. He says: 'Revisiting old haunts, eh?'

'Yes . . . .' I scan his face for any clue, and find nothing.

His mouth opens in a jovial bud. 'Getting over it all right, eh?'

'Sure.' Does everybody know about me, then? Did I have a breakdown in the observatory, streak down the village street?

Then he says: 'Don't you recognise me?' A faint hurt mitigates his coarseness, and I feel ludicrously sorry. At the same time there erupts in me an inexplicable levity, as if I were drunk.

'Now let me see : . . .' I pretend to study him, stand back, chin cupped in hand. 'Brogue shoes . . . golf-club tie . . . . You look like a chartered surveyor to me . . . .'

He roars with laughter and claps my shoulder. 'So you're back on form! Splendid! What about a drink?'

'Later, later, maybe I'll look in.' I pull away and he nods and half raises his arm in aborted good-will. I venture: 'Remember me to your wife.'

'I will, I will!' And he turns back to the pub.

This foolish euphoria accompanies me down the lane to her flat. A few lights are shining in other windows, and people are locking up their garages. Then all at once, before the house edges into view, my heart is booming and the fever burns behind my eyes. She may be away, she may be living with someone else, she may be anywhere. I sit down on a garden wall and wait until the faintness passes. My own frailty frightens me: I don't know how it happened. Then I get up and pat my hair into place like someone going for an interview, and my feet falter over the tarmac.

But her windows are empty. They're somehow ghastly: rectangles of black, curtainless. I cross the lane to them, longing for any sign of life. But I see only the glimmer of the psychopath's light on the floor above. I peer through the glass into the sitting-room, and the glow of a distant street-lamp faintly dispels its dark. The landlord's leather chairs and sofa, the fake antique table and desk, are almost all that's left. Some silver spotlights are dimly visible above. I think I can make out on the walls the hooks and the ghostly rectangles where her pictures and posters once hung.

I go round to the back, and the bedroom is curtainless too. There's no light to illumine its interior. I try to imagine her belongings re-arranged in some other pattern, some other room, perhaps amongst a man's. But instead an emptiness fills me. I can't feel my feet as they walk over the lawn. A breeze could blow me away. Out here the world has turned very small. The stars have gone. Even the trees look evanescent, and this pain in me is a long way off. A lurid urban glow reddens the night clouds on the horizon. I'd never noticed that before. Where has she gone? I return to the front door by habit, and peer through the letter-box. The mat beneath is splashed with envelopes. I cannot read them. Then, I don't know why, I press the doorbell. It sounds far inside, scratching the silence with a desolate tingling, and deepens the emptiness. And the next moment, in a helpless upheaval of my body, I'm weeping. I swear out loud at myself – after all, she's only gone somewhere else – but I lean in the doorway and these spasms come retching out of me, as if I'm saying farewell.

It is a long time before I wrench myself away. I walk up and down the lawn fast, clearing my head. I turn my face back and forth in the cold breeze, like water. After a minute a window opens on the upper storey and a man's face appears. He is dishevelled, suspicious. He sounds hoarse, as if he rarely speaks: 'What do you want?'

'I'm looking for Miss Everard.' The words echo lonely in the silence.

The man does not answer, only stares down. After a moment he fumbles with the window-latch, preparing to withdraw. My voice comes louder, tense: 'Where is Jaqueline Everard?'

In the faint lamp-light, I see him smile. Then he draws his levelled hand across his throat.

He's mad, of course. She said herself he was a psychopath. I'm trembling partly because it's cold. These people should be institutionalised. The observatory will tell me where she's gone. But I can't face my supervisor or the others in this state, not without my mind, not yet. What a farce. After all, I could have picked up the telephone and talked to her that way, if she'd been here. But I wanted to see her in the flesh.

18

I can't recall Sandra's street at first, and when I look her up in the telephone directory there are too many under 'Smith, S'. So I return to the lane where I glimpsed her sipping coffee in the café window, then retrace our steps until I find her door. It is painted a jolly pink, and 'Rosie' and 'Sandra' are inscribed above the bell-button, as if they were call-girls. (But they're not: this is only their innocence.)

When I try to picture Sandra, she becomes your ghost. It's just weakness, I know, wanting to come to her like this, so late (it's almost ten o'clock) and with nothing to say. But it's as if she were in some way your shadow. My finger quivers weakly on the doorbell. I can't stop trembling. It is only four days since I met her, but it seems so long ago that I'm afraid she's become somebody else. More likely, after how I treated her before, she'll slam the door on me. But even then I will have seen your shadow.

Then it opens, and it's Sandra. For an instant I don't exactly recognise her. She is as I remember, but her features are taking time to settle. They've detached themselves from Jaqueline's, and become more puckish and fragile. Even the short, backswept hair and grey eyes are those of a stranger: the hair fairer than Jaqueline's, the eyes less consuming.

She says: 'Oh, it's you!' The door jerks under her hand, as if she might close it. She stares. 'You look awful.'

'I've driven quite a way,' I mumble. 'I'm sorry. It's too late.'

'Come on in then.' Her green high-heels clatter up the stairs in front of me. I remember her legs. Heavy Metal is playing in the sitting-room, and dead joss-sticks circle the postcard Buddha. Rosie is out. The room has the scented snugness of somewhere occupied all evening. She boils an electric kettle while looking at me in slight awe. 'Are you okay? Has something happened?'

'Nothing. Nothing's really happened.' I can't think what to say to her. I should never have come. I don't know what I was expecting to find. But whatever it was, it's not in this room, this bemused girl. She has nothing to do with anything mine. She is Sandra Smith, separate, a solicitor's secretary in Dorchester. 'I'm sorry. I shouldn't be intruding on you. I'm just . . . overworked.'

She says: 'Oh, have you discovered something new? Have you found a new planet?' She holds out a mug of coffee. 'Why are you laughing?'

But my laugh sounds sickly and old to me.

She says: 'What's the point if you don't discover something?'

'Well, none, I suppose . . . .'

She says rather soberly: 'I hope you haven't found any more black holes?'

My laugh sounds more robust this time. 'No, one's enough.'

She hesitates either to settle beside me on the sofa or to perch on a separate chair. In the end she sits down on the carpet near me, hugging her knees, while her coffee diffuses warmth through me. But I think: after ten minutes, I must go. Because this is wrong, my arrival here is a lie. I say: 'Haven't you got a boyfriend, Sandra?'

'Not right now.' She leans back on her elbows, crossing her legs in front of her. 'But I'd rather have none than Rosie's. I'm okay on my own.' She looks at me quizzically, remembering our first evening, I think, and floats out a smile. 'What about you?'

Perhaps from shame at how I treated her, a sense of owing her something, or perhaps from the simple urge to confess, I say: 'Sandra, last week I lost my memory.'

'Oh I often do that.'

'No, I mean properly, completely. I seem to have drifted about for two days, and when I came to, I couldn't remember a thing for nearly two years back. They were just a blank. Most of it's come back now, in bits, but not all.'

I thought this might alarm her, but instead she climbs onto the sofa beside me. 'That's fascinating,' she says. 'Where do you think your memory went?'

'I think it's just suppressed.'

'You don't think it goes anywhere?' The slanted eyes are staring into mine, concerned, ignited. I find it hard to meet them. She says: 'I think I'd lose my memory too in your job, thinking of all the light-years and that. In a way there wouldn't be much point in a memory, would there? I think I'd just go on gazing up.'

'It's more like mathematics, I'm afraid. You need your memory.' I want to put my hand on her knee, but don't. 'I have to tell you this, Sandra. I know it sounds crazy, but when I first saw you, I imagined you were the girlfriend I'd forgotten.

That's why I was so strange with you.'

Her expression does not change. 'Have you remembered her now?'

'Yes.'

She makes a little 'Oh' of disappointment.

I think it is her eyes which are haunting. When they're interested, they become Jaqueline's. I say: 'This girl and I must have split up. But I don't remember why.'

'Can't you ask her?'

'It's not the same as remembering.' Yet memory is what I'm afraid of. So long as I don't feel it, so long as it's only a collection of facts, I can cope. 'I don't want to see her with half a brain.'

Her uncanny eyes go on watching me. She says: 'Are you scared?'

'Yes.' I must be looking ghastly.

Her hand comes up and strokes my cheek, gently, a little theatrically. But she looks puzzled. 'What are you scared of?'

'I don't know.' There's just this panic when I think of her, of what she might inflict, of what lies under the fog of my amnesia. Now that so much memory is rushing in (only an hour ago an image returned of Jaqueline mimicking my father) I feel naked. Things press up under my skull, which has grown very thin. I can't help following Sandra's face in its little flexions and intensities, and am ashamed of what I dream there. I'm not sure if she just pities me. The hand which still caresses my cheek seems platonic, but her thigh is pressing against mine. I reach up and touch her hair with its lights.

She says: 'D'you still love her?'

But I don't trust this word any more. I don't know what it means (I used to). I can say: I'm

178

afraid of you, I long for you, I'm impassioned by you, I half hate you. But 'love'? I don't know where these other feelings come from. They break out of me as if I were a little mad. Perhaps they are just a mania, and not about her at all, but myself. 'Love her?' I stare into the grey eyes. 'I don't know.'

She sounds quite cross. 'You hardly know anything!'

Her hand is on my thigh now. Her hair glitters in my fingers, against my lips. This is terrible, this is what I was not going to do. An act of theatre, of cowardice. But it's like dying back into myself, all the pressure diffusing. Her face unfocuses, becomes a dream of cheekbones and eyes. I kiss these eyes shut – it's my last effort to deflect them – but they open at once, and their lashes flicker on my lips. Her mouth stops my trembling. And I don't know how long I drink from this deep, resolving wholeness, on and on, almost without movement, and it gives an illusion of my entering somewhere more precious than itself, redirecting the past.

Then I feel the scratch of her rings against my neck as she breaks away. 'Phew, I'm out of breath!' But she sees my face, kisses me again. She says: 'You can take me if you like.' I look back at her, dazed. She's become herself. Her hand lingers on my neck. She says: 'I fancy you. I'm feeling hot.'

I cannot tell how much this is true and how much springs from compassion – her fingers are stroking my face again. Perhaps she does not know, either. And perhaps these mannerisms, which suggest she is playing a game, are natural to her. But I try to shake the sickness from my head.

And I know I daren't accept her. I'd descend into a room of mirrors. I don't want to hurt her, but my gratitude sounds clumsy and formal, and I end: 'I want to, Sandra, but it wouldn't be enough.'

But I know that it is not only for her that I'm leaving. It's for my own sanity. I must calm myself, integrate. Maybe, too, I am keeping the illusion of her a little intact, unbroken by some final knowledge. I've become a harmless coward.

Then, from the hall beneath us, we hear a door grate open and the sound of voices. 'That's Rosie.' Quickly she wets her finger on her lips and dabs my cheek – 'Lipstick!' – and I thank her.

Do dreams, I wonder, escape amnesia? Can you dream what you've forgotten?

Tonight, my sleep is bathed in smoke, and I see Jaqueline standing on the volcano's edge. She spreads out her arms as if she owns it. I call: 'Watch out! It's crumbling!'

Always in my dreams the fears which I formulate materialise. Yet as the ground gives way she does not fall but dives and circles below me like a bird of prey. I see her back and outspread arms growing dimmer in the vapour, while she says something I cannot hear. I stay rooted to the ground. At last she dwindles to a spark, like a satellite caught by the sun, and vanishes in the steam which is perhaps her own breath.

I cry after her, not because she is in pain or drowning, but because she is leaving me, and wake up dry-throated, dry-eyed, with Naomi's hand on my wrist. 'You've been dreaming, it's just a dream.'

19

I never liked the place. Too plain, too dark. It was only lit by her. Even the lawn and flower-beds looked municipal. In winter the trees thinned away from pylons and a housing-estate. She said: 'It's a stepping-stone', and yanked the curtains across the view. But a stepping-stone to what, I didn't dare ask.

She said: 'Do you want to go out?'

'No, let's stay.' It was our last evening that I remember. Our times had grown fewer. She made excuses and I couldn't bear them. I gave up asking her.

'Yes, it's starting to rain. Let's eat here.'

Gratitude even for the stilted words now, for anything in her company, but my presence turning her stony. Her silence made my voice squeak in it. I talked to stop her saying something irredeemable: we should end this.

You've reduced me so deeply, so subtly. I've hardly noticed it happen. You walk about me with purpose. Into the sitting-room, out of the bathroom, into the kitchen, while I sit paralysed, furious, unable to touch you. What's happened to us.

She tugged open the fridge door. It's stuck with postcards and snapshots: undergraduate faces backed by quads and college gardens. Past boyfriends, some of them. But they had no discernible common denominator. Was I her type? I don't know. But I was not yet stuck on the door. I used to think it good that she retained the memory of her loves on her fridge. But then I wasn't sure. They might have been notched up like game. Even James, the one before me. In his photograph he had his arms around her. She pulled out cottage pie and lettuce, slammed them all shut.

I asked suddenly: 'Why did you get rid of James?' I was trying to anticipate something. For the first time I felt sorry for him.

She said: 'Because he started smoking after we'd made love.'

'No, seriously. Why?'

She didn't smile. 'Don't you think that's serious? Think about it.'

I thought about it, but nothing much occurred to me, beyond distaste. Perhaps the man was a chain-smoker.

'Think. The pleasure-principle rampant. The sheets stank.' She opened the fridge door again. 'I've still got your old wine.'

Then she talked with a hard, concentrated clarity, about her work, her status in the observatory, her future. It was like a manifesto, yet I scarcely remember it at all, only her. Stone-grey eyes fixed at some point beyond me, the timbre of her voice, and my own head seething with pathetic rancour. She might as well have been alone.

I go into the studio. Naomi is not there. Why is she never there when my memories return? It's full of evening light. On the easel is the portrait of an imagined woman. Nearby lies the postponed sketch of me. I am still an outline waiting to be filled. I have no face.

I remember her saying: 'The reaction to a portrait I most cherish is shock, then recognition, then pensiveness. After that I feel I may have done my job.'

I want her definition of me now.

Soon afterwards I hear her return. She's depressed, the canvas of a London solicitor still under her arm. She says: 'It would be disgusting to please people like that.' She gives a rueful laugh.

I say: 'Perhaps he recognised himself.' I try to laugh too, but my voice is haggard with these returning presences. Perhaps she does not notice, or perhaps she does. You cannot tell with her.

It came at midday: the packet from Palomar Observatory which would confirm (or refute) that the zone where my black hole lay was unoccupied by a star. I put it in my pocket like an unexploded bomb. At these moments I'm no good. On one hand I felt sure that the computations of a year and a half had built up a watertight case. Yet these calculations – all the intricate and fastidious structure of numbers – lived like nuns in their own dimension. Against a simple image of the night sky, they seemed suddenly irrelevant. A report from the duty astronomer at Palomar was attached, but it gave only a standard log: time, weather, moon. There was no one sitting near my work-station when I returned and slid the disc into my display unit. As the image came up, I could hardly confront it. I pictured so clearly some unknown star glimmering where my black hole should lie, that I was afraid I had willed it onto the screen. But instead, as I looked, I saw that the zone showed a blessed nothingness. There, where the dark star lay, was a sheet of black night, beautiful.

For two hours I absorbed this wonder while I eliminated from the picture all trace of cosmic interference, and at last produced a false-colour image where only the companion star – a red supergiant – glowed confidently in the place where it should be. For a moment I remained seated, nursing an exhausted triumph. Then I folded the chart like a keepsake in my wallet and went to find Jaqueline.

I discovered her walking under the trees in the garden where the inaccurate sundial stood. She was eating a sandwich. Later I remembered that this was where ten months ago I had first seen her, laughing at time, and our reunion here took on a sad symmetry. But for the moment, before I even reached her, I pulled the chart from my pocket and shouted: 'I've got it!'

She was smiling non-committally. 'Got what?'

'The photograph from Palomar!'

'Show me.' She put out a hand, unfolded the picture and held it away from her. I remember how she concentrated, how all her features seemed to be pointing at it like a firing-squad. But it was a professional scrutiny, intent, expression-less. Then she handed it back and said: 'That must have pleased you.'

I returned it to my wallet. 'But what do you think?'

'It's not my project.' She offered me a sandwich. 'It seems fine.'

'Jaqueline, can't you say anything more than that?' The desire to please her, or to salvage our intimacy, sank under a surge of anger. 'It's the culmination of my work and that's all you have to say!'

'Oh come on, Edward. It's only optical confirmation. It was a foregone conclusion.' She was watching me with the contained cynicism I hated. 'You finished the real work weeks ago.'

'And you never noticed.' It's true, she never did. Never thought, never asked. Just talked about other things. 'Anybody would think you were jealous.'

But I knew that it was not this. Nothing so simple or human, nothing so comforting. Perhaps it was because certainties unsettled her. That dry, irritated laughter. They reeked of security, which she despised or could not believe. Even now – staring at her in fury – I loved her glittering difference. She appalled me. There was a chasm where belief should be.

She said: 'Why should I be jealous? What does it mean in the end, another black hole candidate? Not much.' I remember her look then, so empty, so scathing. I could have hit her. 'You know as well as I do, we're living in the Stone Age of science. A century ago who'd have believed that gravity could bend light, or electrons jump about? And what now? Cosmologists are guessing that the universe has not four, but eleven or twelve different dimensions. Yet you imagine you're discovering reality, Edward, you even speculate about time reversing – is that because you want to reverse death? – and all the while we're dealing in mirages.'

I tried to calm my voice to the caustic detachment of hers. But it dwindled into meanness. 'Then your own project is as pointless as all the rest.'

'Yes, it's a game. It's *fun*.' She tossed up her paper bag and dropped it over the blade of the sundial. 'And anyone who thinks it's anything more is an infant.'

'But what else do we have to be going on with? Why despise temporary measures?'

'Oh, I don't!' She laughed airily. 'I love them! They're everything!' She plucked the bag from the sundial, exposing its faulty shadow, but her voice turned harsh, impatient. 'Listen. Can you imagine a finite universe? No, because you ask what must be beyond it. But can you imagine an infinite universe? No, because you ask where it must end. The trouble is that natural selection has formed our brains to cope with space and time in the world of the village tom-tom.' She patted the sundial, then started back for the observatory. 'Why are you looking like that? It's not my fault!'

But if I was looking stricken, in the end, it was because I knew that we were not really arguing about dimensions or infinity, or only a little, but that I was saying: *Why don't you love me any more?*

And she was answering: *Why don't you leave me alone?*

In the orchard outside the window old sunlight leaks between the trunks. The blossom has turned brown in the grass. All in a week. If the wind is still, I can hear the booming of the sea. And because everything seems to remind me of something now, it unnerves me. I wander into the kitchen, where I cannot hear it.

For no special reason I decide to telephone my father, and am surprised to be answered by the voice of a woman. I recognise the tones of his wholesome-looking neighbour with bobbed hair. She says: 'Your father won't be back for two hours. He's gone to a meeting in the village, Eddy.' My nickname wobbles on her lips. I dislike it there.

But I am glad, for him, that my mother's void is finding a partial occupant. His loneliness would have grown unbearable. As for my mother, if she has a voice, it is encouraging him to marry again.

All the same, I feel drawn into sad league with her. I cannot quite forgive him. She seems to be buried deeper now, to have slipped down deeper into time, farther away.

We moved onto the gravel path to the observatory. I said: 'So you'll spend your life playing games?'

She thought I meant astronomy, and said: 'Certainly! What else is there?' She touched my shoulder, but condescendingly, a sort of pat. 'It can't be more than a game, can it?' Then she stopped, her eyes on me, suddenly serious. 'Edward, we can't get out of our skins, so the universe is unknowable. Isn't it? Deeply, I mean. Particles change behaviour the instant they're observed. So how can we know what they normally do? Quantum scientists are even starting to say that the act of observation itself brings them into being, that the universe only exists because we're looking at it. Without observers, there would be no universe.' She was kicking at the gravel. If she had any religion, I realised, it was this. She could believe in everything, or nothing. There was no difference.

I said dully: 'Does that make us unimportant?' I meant suffering, love. Why did she always reduce me to this?

'*More* important, I expect.' She was grinning again, a cutting levity. 'The Plains Indians thought the stars came down and spoke to them.'

'I meant *us*.' *Are you dead to me? Have you already gone?*

'It just means we don't understand.' She let out her abrasive laugh. 'Do you see me clearly? Am I here only because you're looking?'

Sometimes I think she means to push me over the edge. Her hand came up to pat my cheek. I put it away. We were at the observatory entrance now. She doesn't mean to destroy, I think. It's something she can't help and doesn't notice. I know she exists, because I couldn't have invented her.

It's dark now. Naomi is in her studio. I go back to my study and rummage through drawers whose jumbled articles and notes I have not sorted. They are no more familiar than when I first read them a week ago. But I recognise them for what they are: the detritus of my breakdown. Only some of the calculations make more sense now than they did, but others are lunatic, and I still cannot remember writing any of them.

It's the notebook I return to, with its apocalyptic ravings. They peter out in random jottings and fragments of stellar myth. The scientific data disappears and the jagged handwriting sometimes slips off the page altogether. I might have been drunk. The excerpts sometimes come from books I don't recall. They appear in different inks and moods. It's like an obsessional commonplace book. But I still don't know what uprooted me. I can't have been so frail. Look at these scribblings. She might have been composing them in my head. But the handwriting is a crazed variant of my own. My supervisor must be laughing.

'Galileo said "*Nature nothing careth whether her reasons be, or be not, exposed to the capacities of men.*" We just remake the world in our own image. For ever. Naomi: the outer world used to begin at my fingertips. But not any longer, not now. It starts in my retina and mind. It's only a mirror. You know that Matisse poster of *The Artist and his Model* hanging in your studio, the sitter clothed, the painter naked? So you understand.

The horrid doubt always arises, (wrote Darwin) *whether the convictions of a man's mind, which has developed from the mind of the lower animals, are of any value, or at all trustworthy? Would anyone trust the convictions of a monkey's mind?*

Our minds may thus resemble the sea shell, which when placed to the ear sounds as if it echoed the murmuring of the waves, and yet the murmur is nothing but the murmur of our own blood . . . . Who then will keep watch upon this watcher, or stand sponsor for his fidelity?
                                    The Human Situation.

This house has been in ruins since eternity.
                                    Samhadi.

The first usable telescope which Kepler received from Elector Ernst of Köln (who in turn had received it from Galileo) showed the stars as squares *and intensely coloured.*

The stars are the vertebrae of the night animal in whose stomach we live. They are the night's backbone.

The darkness moves with them, prowling like a lion.
Without them, the blackness would fall down in pieces
on our heads.

Botswana belief.

She comes in and hesitates behind my chair, then puts her arms round me. This surprises me, but I don't mind. She says: 'You're going through all that.'

'Have you read it?'

'You showed it to me once.'

I wonder why, and what more she knows. 'Was I wretched when I wrote it, or crazy, or what?'

'You were looking for peace.' Her arms release me.

'So you see, Jaqueline, I did listen. I used to imagine Einstein's time and space were a curved perfection out there. I know better now. In a way you healed me from the grief of appearances.

Winds and cold stream over the earth from gaps in the
tent-roof of the sky. The pillar supporting the sky is the
tethering-post of the stars which wander.

Siberian belief.

The rulers of the Ottoman empire would banquet in
tulip gardens, roamed by tortoises with candles on their
backs. To the inebriate sultans, these wandering flames
merged with the night sky above the Bosphorus to
become the stars.

Facts alone are not strong enough for making us
accept, or reject, scientific theories, the range they leave
to thought is too wide; logic and methodology elimi-
nate too much, they are too narrow. In between these

190

*two extremes lies the ever-changing domain of human
ideas and wishes.*

Feyerabend.

*There is amongst the Hebrews a writing which they
call Celestiall, because they shew it placed and figured
amongst the stars.*

Henry Cornelius Agrippa.'

I want to hear a human voice. Automatically I
ring Sandra. She sounds as if she has just emerged
from sleep, but says: 'You caught me doing meditation.'

'What were you thinking about?'

'You don't think. That's the point. My guru says
you must concentrate on the gaps between
things.'

I say ruefully: 'I'd be good at that.'

'Oh, haven't you got your memory back then?'

My thoughts start to blunder. 'More of it comes
all the time. . . . But unhappy things seem to hang
back. I suppose the mind is hoping they'll go away
or aren't really there.'

'The mind's funny.'

'Yes.'

Her voice turns plaintive, embarrassed. 'Do you
think, Edward . . . when you've remembered her
properly, you'll go back to her?'

'It may be too late.'

The words come out quite easily, but now they
are there they take on a tormenting solidity. Her
voice goes on chirruping in the receiver, but I can
only distantly answer it. My hands are trembling.
Under them the notebook excerpts tumble down
the pages, ripped from primitive cosmology,

anthropologists' reports, African myth, even Toraja songs from Sulawesi.

'One of the hunters saw a seal. On the nape of its neck was a ball of fire. He speared it, and the seal swam seaward and dragged his canoe up into our sky. The other hunters know about this, because they all saw them going up and sticking in the sky, in the place where the stars are.

The never-vanishing stars row the sun-god across the sky by day. But at night they are the grandchildren of Isis, and their meadows form the habitations of the blessed dead.

Sun, moon and stars are gold the gods hang in the eyes of those on earth to daze them. They are the ideas of the gods.

We are as the phantoms of this world;
the apparitions of this religion,
as the wind that blows along the house.'

20

She pretended to be asleep last night when I came so late to bed, and this morning she looks tired. She dresses in the bathroom and returns only to tie back her hair and momentarily to smooth her fingertips over her cheeks in the mirror. For a few minutes I lie in bed, feeling dulled and listening to the clink of pots in the kitchen. Then I wait for the blasting in the quarry to begin, as if it must summon memories again. But nothing sounds. Sometimes I imagine that the blank wall at which these memories end may be easing apart, but I cannot tell if the stray images which erupt in me are make-belief, and I close my eyes to them.

The morning is comforting in its ordinariness, cloudy and cool. I make my way to the kitchen in the dressing-gown which was Naomi's gift, and join her at breakfast for the first time. In the week since my return we have both avoided this, as if it would project too great an intimacy onto the day ahead, but now we tinker sleepily with plates and bowls, and settle opposite one another at the pine table. I watch her movements with a curious, warm pleasure, the way her fingernails click against her cup, her comical clasping of the sides of her head when she yawns.

'Are you going back to paint the solicitor?'

'No, that's over.'

'I hope he paid you.'

She says: 'He offered, but I refused.'

'He wasted your time.'

'I expect he feels I wasted his.' She gets up and crosses to the stove. Sometimes she has a habit of splaying out her feet as she walks, like a domestic ballerina, as if she were asserting ownership of the kitchen. She returns with an egg which she has fried hard in a way she likes: she hasn't faced a soft egg since contracting hepatitis at the age of seventeen. 'What are you staring at?'

'Just you and your egg.' I don't know why this amuses me, and nor does she. She toys with it. I feel there's something displaced between us, but I can't locate it.

She says: 'Do you want cereal or just bread?' She's moved to the sideboard now. 'Why are you laughing?'

'Oh, just at you.' I am laughing at the odd, sweet blurring of her r's, which used to happen only when she was tired. (I'm sure she didn't sleep.)

'You're in a funny mood this morning.' But she's smiling, restless. She goes over to the geraniums in the alcove orangery and waters them with a kettle. I think how I will spend the day: a week before my sick-leave ends. She returns with toast and pours me coffee, sits down again. I watch the fastidious way she pares the crusts from her toast. Her fingers look double-jointed. Their cuticles are lined with oil-paint. She opens a pot of bitter marmalade, sniffs it, and starts to spread its contents with preoccupied flickers of her knife. I wonder why she doesn't eat honey any more.

'You used to like honey.'

'Yes.' I see her suddenly blush and stare down.

Then she darts me a look of weirdly mixed elation and alarm. I can't decipher her. She begins to bolt down the toast as if its marmalade were crucial, then gets to her feet. She says: 'I'm going out. I want to walk.'

I follow her to the door. 'What's wrong?'

'Nothing's wrong.' She stoops to tug on some gumboots. I stand beside her nonplussed. As she bends, the curve of her spine shows beneath her blouse in an arc of delicate vertebrae, and I walk my fingers up them like the march of a goblin. It's just an excuse for touching her, of course (it always was), but she swivels round and stares at me. Her face opens in a kind of radiant disbelief. She breathes: 'You always used to do that.'

'Yes, of course.'

'You remember.'

I stare back at her, into the dark eyes, the full mouth, and I'm aware of gazing into a sea of familiarity, of the return of something so natural that it must have slid back unnoticed minutes ago. I stare on and on at her. Behind her face a thousand remembered versions of itself are crowding in, a whole history, so that it seems physically to fluctuate and fill, to diversify in shifting contours, tiny skin blemishes, quivers of past expression. Yet she just gazes back. And when we embrace it is with this trembling tentativeness, as if too much movement will throw us back off balance.

After a while we sit down in the orangery, exhausted, I in the high-backed chair, she in the patinated one. I'm still in my dressing-gown, she in her gumboots. I reach out and clasp her arm. For the first time I feel sure of who it is I am holding. But I have an idea that if I let go she will stiffen and withdraw again behind her mask. We talk almost in whispers, afraid of disturbing each other's presence. Once or twice, when she articulates an unexpected thought or her hands make a forgotten gesture, I feel as if I'm falling in love with her all over again. At other times it is like dropping into a warm bath. Expressions which sounded trivial or meaningless before I recognise as the private language of our love, and an aureole of even comic memories attaches itself to her. I watch her, listen. Half an hour ago the same opinions and intuitions, the same gestures and cadences, made only faint impressions on me. Now it is as if some infusion has steeped her in a complexity and charm whose change must surely, I feel, have happened outside my head.

Yet I think uncomfortably: how strange, only the past seems to hold any power for me. Naomi's face needed its history, my remembrance, in order to come fully alive. Now I am afraid that I have lost the capacity to feel, or even believe in, anything new. The past may nourish the present; but the future does not exist.

Maybe that is why I observe her, as I wish I had observed my mother before her death, in case she should escape again into the death of no memory. This fear of loss is my hell. I remember trying to seal Jaqueline in an erotic chrysalis, or in a definitive photograph among the tombs of Sulawesi. And that is how I look at Naomi now, remembering (while I can) the beauty of which you are unaware (your face unmade-up, your hair in an elastic-band). These are the wide-set eyes, soft but uncompromising, and the mobile mouth which only a fluke of memory recovered. I feel like labelling them. And the strangeness is (I know, you told me) that my loving changed your expression a little, softened it. I am looking at my own creation.

She says: 'But you don't recall everything.'

No, I don't. My last memories lap against the time eight weeks ago when I began to decline. And in all these recovered months Jaqueline keeps her island of oblivion, as if I were trying to exclude her. But of course I have no control, and I know she will resurrect, everything will come back, my mind seems in splinters. I say: 'No, not everything.' But I think she knows this. 'Don't let's talk about it. I'm frightened of adding even to the memories of you.' Yet my head in my hands only makes an ugly darkness and I look up again in case she has gone. But her arm returns beneath my fingers and she is gazing with that steadiness which in arguments (I remember several) I have come to respect.

Now she crouches between my knees and rests her elbows there, and says: 'You may regret your memories of me, because I stood back as you grew weaker. It seemed presumptuous to console you, to try to feel what you were feeling. Maybe I sometimes seem hard because I'm trying not to be stupid, I don't know.' She rests her cheek on my knee. 'But I failed you.'

I can't deny this because I can't remember, or I don't want to. I want to forget. I want to stay in this moment. Perhaps it is her rested cheek which touches me with a sense of her fragility, in spite of all she says, and a memory of us walking last December through the quarries above the sea.

It was bitterly cold. We entered the earth-floored galleries without a torch, and found a bat hanging like a tulip from the ceiling. I remember

197

Naomi's eyes in the dark, wide open and wondering if it might have died in its sleep. Then we came to the pillars of living rock covered in graffiti. Whimsically I hunted for anything to carve with, and found a discarded nail. The stone was hard and slippery. I wonder why I failed to notice this blazon on my return, but perhaps I never carved it deep enough. I began with a flamboyant E, planning to twine it with a graceful N. But somewhere on the E's downstroke the nail snapped and gouged an inch-long trench across my wrist.

Naomi wound her scarf around it, then noticed a rusty fragment embedded under the blood. She led me into the light. She said: 'I'm going to get that out.'

I remember her voice's coolness as she picked a pair of tweezers from her bag. Her thumb and middle finger closed over the wound. Then she said: 'This'll hurt. Close your eyes.' I closed them and waited. Several seconds went by. 'Keep them closed.' But covertly I looked, and saw her hand trembling against her cheek. Then she picked the fragment out.

Perhaps what I most love in her, she despises.

Now I flick back my sleeve and glimpse the dog-leg scar still livid on my wrist. Odd how I never noticed it. It is as if the unremembered becomes invisible.

Naomi has got up and is tidying the cupboards, singing softly to herself. I watch her indulgently. She is thinner than two months ago, perhaps because of my decline. Even when at ease, her movements are fluent and economical; only when I first knew her she wore her hair loose, and she retains a beguiling habit of sweeping back vanished strands from her cheeks.

I go over to help her wash up. I feel like a patient, fragile, altered, and I still cannot understand that she, of course, is unchanged. But as I move round the house its artefacts age and settle round me. Memory revalues them, and objects which were alien before – ownerless shapes and colours – revert and glow in their old perspective. The house becomes alive with intimacies, mutual gifts. Here we whitewashed a wall, there we hung a curtain. I look to see if she still keeps her tights in a shoe-box (she does), and her bedside photographs no longer depict strangers but her parents, whom we've sometimes visited. Yet other objects remain stubbornly blank. My own study depresses me – it's redolent of too much solitude – and in her studio several canvases which I recall her painting stay mute to me: too cerebral, too chill. But then I'm a visual Philistine, she says.

When I return to the kitchen, conscious of her moving around me, I think how little, even now, I know her. I never studied her. I was too obsessed with my work. I think she rather liked that: it suited her reticence. But if recovery means returning to that callousness, I'd rather stay frail. I long to make amends, and I wonder again what shaped her: what incited her passion to paint, her difficult integrity, even her taste for certain herbs and flowers, for chunky pullovers and lambskin gloves, her bursts of humour.

After a minute I touch my fingertips against her blouse above the heart, and her hand echoes this against mine. It's something we used to do: like making sure of one another's existence, beating with the same rhythm, or nearly. I say: 'I never gave you enough thought.'

She laughs. 'You did. You've forgotten!'

But all the time I'm conscious that she's listening to me with a tremulous waiting, as someone might watch an apparently healthy patient for the first sign of a cancer that's incurable. I fancy that her heart accelerates under my hand. She doesn't meet my gaze (and that's unlike her) but seems to be saying to herself: *he doesn't know, he doesn't know*.

I relinquish her. She guesses: 'It's coming back, isn't it?'

'Yes.'

'Let it.'

I want to let it, but it's a ghastly confusion. I say: 'Don't worry.' I hover into a chair, facing the orchard, the disintegrated blossom. 'Leave me alone with it.'

Of course there are clichés galore: time heals, memory fades. She doesn't offer them, but for a second her fingers squeeze my wrist, stroking its scar, then she goes quickly out.

The fever has started, my old enemy, throbbing between my eyes. How long have I known this? But I don't even know it now, not properly, not sequentially. I heat my hands in my pockets. I'm still in my dressing-gown: a mental patient. Outside, the orchard is full of gulls: a rough sea sends them inland. I wait, and it comes. It feels dull and heavy. It has the mass of a dead star. It could drop through the earth. And when it comes, it comes as her happier memories do, cold, without tears.

I open the window on the orchard. In spite of Naomi, it is as if the present has no validity, as if I have already lived my life and am observing it from the vantage of extreme old age, or even death. Everything has already happened, and will not recur. Nothing again can happen. I know this insults her (but she is not in the room) and that it will not last. But for the moment the past eliminates all future.

21

We watched the clusters of Perseus and Auriga sharpen out of the evening sky. For August, it was cold. A few row-boats were rotting in the cove, and we sat on these while we waited. I don't remember how she looked. I seemed to be in a daze with her. On the rocks above us hung a line of dour cottages with names like Tide's Reach and The Ark. They showed no lights. From their gateposts rotting gangways dropped vertically to the shingle, their lower rungs starched in sea-weed, and mooring ropes looped down to the boats.

Neither of us had dived by night before. We must have booked weeks in advance, or I think we would have cancelled. We had lost the art of speech together. After a few minutes she got up and began pacing up and down the shingle. She seemed irritated by the cold. She said: 'Christ, whose idea was this?'

I said: 'Not mine.' Because it was hers. I've gone over this in my head again and again, and it was hers. It was the kind of thing she loved. I did not even know you could dive in Cornwall. She came back and sat on the prow of the row-boat. I think she was shivering.

'When's this motor cruiser coming?'

'He said in twenty minutes.'

We waited while the far shore of the estuary

scattered into lights. The sky showed a cold brilliance of stars. We had last sat like this in the hot nights of Sulawesi, and I nearly reminded her. But I choked this back, for fear she'd mock it. Instead, in an urge to engage her which I still could not stop, I began talking about mutual passions in astronomy.

She said: 'Sometimes I think this whole thing about black holes will go the same way as phlogiston. People find what they need.'

She knew I'd hate this. She did it on purpose. It was a chance to exercise her mordant anarchy: *the world is a playground. Nothing perhaps exists.* Her head was averted from me, facing the harsh stone wall above the quay. By distancing herself from my work she seemed to be flashing a warning. She added: 'Hulton thinks half the talk is exaggerated, that there's too little evidence.'

Something split in me. I strained to catch her gaze, but her profile was pure marble. I said: 'I don't give a shit what Hulton thinks.'

'He's a bloody good supervisor.' She sounded annoyed, and I was glad. 'Are you getting jealous?'

'Not of that poseur.' But I was, I am. I was jealous of anyone who spoke to her. I was jealous of the shoes she walked in. I can see myself now, so touchy, so truculent, and she goading me on. This is the man I was, may be again. I don't like or even respect him. Angry, volatile, dogmatic: I don't know why any woman ever loved him.

'Black holes have become like God,' she said. 'They pander to people's craving for heaven and hell.' This, in her mocking tone. 'They whisk the universe neatly into a soup of protons and neutrons, and spew it out into another dimension.

Then silly imaginations can endow it with new life, new time, new anything.'

I said: 'I never endowed my project with anything.' It was finished now, and even my supervisor had been pleased. But my future employment was precarious, and she had shown no concern at all. I said: 'You wait till your supernova dies.'

'When it dies,' she said, 'it'll be a useful, straightforward death. It'll tell us something about atmospheric density, then it will disappear into space. It'll be gone. Just a gap in the Large Magellanic Cloud. There'll be no other fancy lessons to be learnt from it. And that's fine by me. When is this damn boat coming?'

I got up to walk. I didn't want to listen to her. But she came alongside me, briskly, without comfort. These were the only moments she paid me attention now, when she had something destructive to say.

She began: 'You always liked those black hole theories: time reversal, white holes leading to anti-universes. Maybe your supervisor was right. You haven't the brain for what you're doing, not the right brain.' She added: 'You should have been a poet,' but there was no affection in her tone.

I thought: she probably thinks even affection sentimental. I said cruelly: 'And you should have been a mortician.'

'No, that would be a job for you. It would make you tougher-minded.'

I was so far past caring I'd turned numb. She's determined I should detest her, I thought, she's telling me to leave. And I can't. I can't. I remember how the lights shone in the water along the quay. We went on walking beyond the shingle. Yes, I detested her. The sand under our feet was printed with the triangles of birds' claws. She said: 'You refuse to face that anything's final,' and I knew what she was leading to. I thought furiously: I'll make it difficult for you, as difficult as I can. If I had the mettle, I'd kiss you, just to make it harder. Those curving lips.

But I said: 'I had to face finality three months ago.' I was ashamed that I'd turned my mother's death into a pawn between us, but it was too late now. 'I've never evaded that. I neither believe, nor disbelieve, in anything beyond death.' But I sounded harrowed, strident. I added bitterly: 'There I agree with you.' Only the difference is, I wish I didn't. I wish I could believe in some kind of redemption. But Jaqueline doesn't wish it. She revels in unbelief.

She said: 'Oh, you do believe, you do. It's in your bones.' She stopped by an iron bollard, rested her arms on it. 'You're a romantic, Edward. Only infinity would satisfy you.' She wore a little smile. 'Well, my father died seven years ago, and he's gone, gone absolutely.' I knew she'd felt nothing for her father, ever; yet she spoke as if our griefs were equal, or perhaps non-existent. She added: 'You don't bring them back by some sleight of mind, you know. They're gone.' She lifted the palm of one hand to her mouth and blew, as if dispelling ash. '*Phut!*'

Then I hated her.

I hated her not for what she disbelieved, but for the indifference with which she disbelieved it. I think in some ghastly way she thought she was helping me, bringing me down to earth. I don't know, I'll never know. I couldn't speak. I just glared at her across the idiot bollard. Her smile faded, not in sympathy, but because she was preparing to move on – I could tell – to that other death, the death of whatever she had once felt for me. Her fingers interlaced over the bollard. I remember thinking even now how fine her eyes were, slanted and pale in the faint light. My fury and grief seemed to silence one another. But it was in petty spite that I got up and walked away from her again, leaving her valediction unsaid. By the time she caught up with me the dive-launch was mooring at the quay.

We climbed in, unspeaking. I've only now remembered that a gull was perched asleep on the cabin roof. Perhaps it was taking refuge from something, like the gulls now wheeling in the orchard beyond the window in front of me. Then the engine coughed into life, and we cast off.

We settled in the stern and picked over our gear. In Sulawesi we'd checked each other's regulators and pressure gauges, less from necessity than affection. Now we just checked our own. I glimpse myself sitting there, a self-obsessed reject complaining about his flippers, and I loathe him. He never gave hers a thought. He just nursed his anger. But it wasn't the equipment at fault, everyone agreed that. Then I remember saying, I hate this, but my last words: 'What's wrong with you, Jaqueline?'

Examining her wet suit, she said: 'I'm sane, that's what's wrong with me.'

We were slipping out of the estuary toward the open sea. Along the headland above us I could make out the serried gables of houses, and a sweep of pines blacker than the sky. The whole estuary glimmered with stagnant lights. In front, over its calm, the waves shifted and rippled like plate-armour. The divemaster stood at the wheel, his back to us. He just said: 'South-east wind. Should be mild.'

The wall of a cargo ship, come to collect china-clay from the wharfs beyond, loomed past us in the estuary mouth. Then the whole inlet, its sleeping yachts and cramped cascade of houses, folded away behind us, and we were out in the dark.

Our motor made a dry stutter over the peace. The divemaster conversed incomprehensibly on the radio, then switched off. He was lean and silent. I felt uneasy in his hands. But ahead of us several buoys were bouncing in the waves, and he knew precisely where to go. A mile from shore we cast anchor above the site where a 3,500-ton pontoon dredger lay on the ocean bottom. It was as big as a football-pitch, the locals said: a favourite summer dive-spot. In 1937 it had turned turtle on the Eddystone Sands and had drifted until its giant buckets scraped the sea-floor, where it broke up.

We struggled into our wet suits by the light of two gas-lamps. I remember thinking how beautiful it was – the sea a metal sheet under the stars. To the divemaster we were just two angry people avoiding one another's eyes. That's all he saw (he later said): a lovers' tiff. He kept his back to us while we dressed. Heavier waves started tugging and slopping under the bows. I remember her lithe body wriggling into the wet suit before she stood for a moment in the stern, her features pared by the constricting hood. And again I feel this yearning to know, to possess, who she was at this moment, even who I was. She was grinning at the sea, suddenly elated, and said to no one in particular: 'This is terrific!' Then I stopped looking at her. I don't think I ever properly looked at her again. I thought I never wanted to.

We sat askew on the boat's edge, while the dive-master fitted our air tanks and buoyancy control jackets. He seemed professional all right. I'd imagined our torches would shine from our heads, but no: we carried them like guns in our hands. I sensed the man knew my inexperience – his partner in the dive-shop had told him. And Jaqueline may have told him too, maybe she did. But I wish now he'd not known.

The wind had hardened, and the water hit us with a shock of cold as we entered it. I was preparing to endure rather than enjoy this. I was doing it to be with her. As I gripped the gunwale rope the waves submerged me and the current tugged my legs horizontal. For an instant, as I surfaced, I saw Jaqueline's head five yards behind me. Her jacket was still inflated, her shoulders clear of the water, her eyes invisible behind her mask. But she seemed to look at me for a second as if asking: are you all right? Yet maybe it was only chance that she faced me like that. Or perhaps I imagined it. It was just an instant. Only later I thought about it, but I can't know, ever, her eyes were in darkness, it's hopeless at night.

Then we descended the anchor rope, the dive-master leading. Our torches dangled blind from our wrists. I felt the pain of unequal pressure in my ears. But twenty feet down the current vanished, as the man said it would, and we fell through a water misted in particles of sand, so that our torch-beams made lonely blades in it, and contacted nothing.

When we hit the bottom there was nothing to be seen there either. Instead of tropical brilliance we moved over a floor of shale and weeds. It might have been a building-site. We glided like ghosts after our torch-beams. She was just behind me. In sunlit waters you float with open vision, but at night we tunnelled like moles into solid matter, pursuing our own light. We could not watch where we were. Instead, it was all around, watching us.

Then we came to where the dredger's scoops lay for a hundred yards over the seabed. They made a barnacled ridge of buckets and stanchions, glazed with weeds, and in their collapse had shed around them a litter of hausers. Ahead of us the divemaster's torch-beam wandered over them. Every half minute he checked that we were following. Behind me Jaqueline's light hoovered across the sand to pick out a starfish or a broken bar, and once I saw, emerging from shale, the massive studlink chain which had powered the whole machine.

I don't know how long we'd been under (time goes quicker underwater). My air gauge was high, maybe we had half an hour to go. But our visibility was shortening. At five yards my torch-beam lost itself in a nebula of fragments, and the divemaster's light, when he turned round, looked stifled and unnatural. He showed us a chamber where air or gas had collected, trapped under the iron ceiling, perhaps for years. I wondered if it had come from the tanks of passing divers, or was the contaminated gas of batteries or of oil. But as the man swam away, Jaqueline – in her voracious curiosity – took out her regulator and breathed it. I was by her side. Immediately she rammed the mouthpiece back, and I thought nothing. Only later, I wonder if it had sickened her. But I didn't know what the vapour was. I don't still. I didn't even look at her. And she was by my side. Yet I remember the iron chamber, and the globules of dead-man's-fingers whitening its ceiling. They seemed to be poking through. And she swam out, she seemed strong. This is terrible. But she seemed strong enough. I might have quickly breathed it myself, to see if it was all right. Just to see. But it wasn't cowardice. I just turned away from what could hurt me: her.

And we laid her out on the quay, and I felt nothing. I carried her myself. There was nothing even to cover her with. He had already telephoned from the boat. I sat there. I kept feeling I'd dislocated my jaw. I couldn't look at her. We saw the blue light of the ambulance reflecting in the streets.

But it may not have been the gas, it may not. The autopsy never revealed that. Because she swam on all right, close behind me, and at last we came to the end, the massive capstan still clean of barnacles. Then we turned into a black forest of stanchions. They circled us in great scoops and ridges. We grazed through the gaps and holes in them. Small fish drifted in their dark. There was a three-foot gear-wheel. I was four yards in front of her, five maybe, still weaving through the superstructure. The divemaster had gone ahead, ten yards. Our torches lit up only these trunks of iron trees. I didn't look behind, not for two or three minutes. Then there was no light behind me. You're meant to team up, divers are. You're responsible for one another. You watch one another. Then I looked back and her torch was wavering up and down. She might have been twenty yards away, which is too far. It looked like a suffocated headlamp. And I did not care. I thought: she's just being clever, investigating every cranny. She's tormenting me again, pushing things to the brink. So, so I . . . . Yes, it occurred to me, yes, she might be in trouble. But it was a half-thought. It didn't even form. It had gone before it formed. So I . . . but I didn't. I didn't. And I, I don't know how long after it was before I looked round again. Maybe two minutes, two. Two. And the divemaster had turned also, in front of me. And there was something odd about her light. It was far away. And my own, as I swam to her, just shining on millions of particles like dead stars in the water.

And I reached her. She was upright, swaying in the current. Her regulator hung loose from her mouth. Her eyes staring in their mask. They didn't look at me. She was drifting free in a wedge of stanchions. Her torch swung from her wrist in the undertow.

And we laid her out on the quay, and I felt nothing. I couldn't even move. I didn't look at her. I didn't care at all, not at all. I had nothing to care with. She might have been a chunk of seaweed. The ambulance seemed to take a century. Two street-lamps shone above the jetty. The coast-guard's flagpole was empty, the wind so low: only the *fluk-fluk-fluk* of its slack cords. The divemaster smoked in his cabin. Her eyes bulged at the stars. We had nothing even to cover her with.

22

The cliffs make an amphitheatre facing the sea. At their foot curves a floor of wave-polished rock. A mist is rolling in. Out to the horizon there's nothing but a damp whiteness. In the inlet there's nothing either, except the arc of cliffs, whose strata have been split and quartered by the wind, so they look artificially assembled. I sit on a ledge, watching her, but I'll never really like the sea again, just get used to it. The stone terraces are cracked like parquet floors. They look as if somebody's scrubbed them. On one side I hear the waves booming into caves, where they turn quiet and auburn before withdrawing.

She is scavenging among the rocks like a student on a project. A dark, slight figure in faded jeans. In this circle of gaunt emptiness, she is finding things. There are no pools, not even weeds. But she lights upon a sea-fern swept in from somewhere else, and a worn mollusc. I wonder if she will add these to her collection, whose artefacts are not obviously attractive, but curious, arresting. But she drops them in the sea. I've forgotten her interest in chance things; or perhaps I never noticed it.

I don't want her to tell me, in a few months: 'You were nicer when you were ill.' So I go over to her and say – it sounds overblown – but I say: 'Remind me to listen to you.'

She says laughing: 'Amnesia's gone to your head.' She's looking where the prismatic foam-bubbles are the only colour in the cove. 'You always listened to me until the last weeks of your decline.'

'Did I seem mad?' Because nobody but Jaqueline existed in my head. It took on a cursed magic: everything she'd ever said, everything I hadn't done.

She says: 'No, just absent. I felt you'd left me a waxwork of yourself, and gone away.'

I say: 'So you painted me.' I still find that hard.

'Yes' – she touches my hand.

We're silent. I think: perhaps that was her way of understanding. The foam drips from the rock-face beside us, and after a minute it splits like old lace. I say: 'I never knew what you thought of her.'

I realise this alarms me. I don't want Naomi to think of her at all. If she thinks of her, Jaqueline will own us both.

Her moment's pause. 'I only know her by what she's done to you.'

And that was the ordeal she transposed to her canvas, of course, in my portrait. Perhaps she painted it in an effort to understand not only me, but Jaqueline. Those scars are the only portrait I have of Jaqueline – a picture of my own pain – because she didn't like even to be photographed. Only one snapshot – of her hated mother – she gave me in jest. But standing in front of the woman, her head barely reaching to her bosom, was a ten-year-old girl. Her hands were clutching each other. In her face the mouth was a tight bud and her eyes contained no hint of their adult blaze, but were caverns of anxiety.

I say: 'Why didn't you tell me she was dead?'

Her hand touches mine again. 'The specialist said your memory would return it when the time was right.'

But sometimes I think the right time is never, and that I can stomach any memory but her light signalling through the water. That's what is unendurable. The only time I ever ignored her. She miscalculated the size of her air tank, it was thought, and became wedged under a stanchion and panicked. She died not by drowning, but by asphyxiation.

I said over and over to the police, the coroner, I should have watched her, I should have watched her. But it was said in such a hard voice, I know, that they looked at me oddly. I sounded soulless. I think I was, then. It was only later that the universe in my head collapsed into somewhere chaotic and terrible. Then there was nothing left but this implacable remembering, and a frailty as if I had no skin, just nerve-ends, like one of those flayed martyrs who went on living for a while. And sometimes I think this may engulf me again, and things will derange, and I'll long to release her from the stanchions, give her my air.

I sit on the rocks, guilty because I'm happy now, without you. But I want you to continue in me (yes, you were right, I have trouble with finality). When I sense you ebbing, I grow more comfortable, but ashamed. (You mock all this, of course, which leaves me lonely.) But you ebb, just the same. Gradually, fitfully. It was nine months ago, after all, and I know your views on death.

I say out loud: 'Of course it was my fault.'

Naomi stands up. She wants me to stand up too. 'You talk as if you murdered her,' she says. 'Just because you were there doesn't make you culpable. You were innocent.'

The word 'innocent' means nothing to me, but because she believes it, it carries a small charge of deliverance, and I smile at her. Under her relief, she carries a faint sadness which I don't yet understand. I say: 'I remember once I did talk to you, about the precariousness and hopelessness of things – the death of the universe – and really I was thinking of her death, and – do you remember? – you just gave me your hand.'

She says: 'What else could I do?'

I don't know, of course. Perhaps I confuse her common sense with wisdom. Last night, in half-sleep, I remembered how two months ago we escaped from the rain into the pagan chapel on the headland. It was dusk, and we only heard the sea. Then an owl alighted on the roof outside and began to hoot incompetently, as if it were learning. We listened in fascination. Her face was glistening with rain. A pot of yellow chrysanthemums, I think, stood on the font. I smelt her woody scent as we kissed. The other smells were dank and noxious here. I remember how the vaulted ceiling took my question about marriage away from us with a dry resonance, as if others were listening. She said: 'Let's wait until you're well.'

It is the remembered, not the forgotten, which threatens us now. In time, perhaps, her profession of my innocence may come to mean something. But not too much. Because whatever happened underwater, my part there stays opaque to me. It unfocuses as I look at it. In a while, I expect, I will find a version which is comfortable to live with, and tell it to myself, until it becomes a kind of truth. Another strangeness of amnesia: that it seems to offer a new beginning, while you long instead for a history, for remembrance. Then when the past returns, the things which you thought would be clear are elusive; yet through their re-remembering they pass into their own reality.

The tide is coming in. The waves pour over the rock-terraces but spend themselves before they reach us. Near our feet the foam subsides to mauve and turquoise beads, which look hard and impermeable among the rocks.

23

Two months later, in the Large Magellanic galaxy beyond the Milky Way, the wreckage of the Sanduleak supernova began to shine again. As it ploughed into its own halo, the heated particles started to glow with a reborn incandescence over an area two light-years across, and radio, X-ray and infra-red signals poured off the explosion. The Hubble Space Telescope recorded the first pictures; then the Parkes radio telescope in New South Wales sent back figures to astronomers in the United States and Britain.

To the naked eye, at first, the supernova was only a ghost growing in the night. Then, for three weeks, it flared into a violent needle of light which was visible even by day. Kalahari herdsmen, noticing the change low on their horizon, thought that a pole had worked itself loose in the canopy of the sky. But in Sulawesi, Toraja elders muttered that God was angry with the young people for no longer burying their dead according to custom.

As the outrush of the dying star reached its climax, other telescopes recorded its changes. They seemed to occur with dazing immediacy, but in fact, because the supernova lay 170,000 light-years away, its disintegration had already taken place long ago, at a time when the last Neanderthals inhabited the earth. After its flare faded even from telescopic sight, only the pulse of its neutron star remained, and its debris floated outward in cooler and ever-thinner clouds, until it diffused into the near-infinite dark.